Thomas Atkins

History of Middlefield and Long Hill

Thomas Atkins

History of Middlefield and Long Hill

ISBN/EAN: 9783337327163

Printed in Europe, USA, Canada, Australia, Japan

Cover: Foto ©Andreas Hilbeck / pixelio.de

More available books at **www.hansebooks.com**

HISTORY

OF

EFIELD and LONG HILL.

BY

Thomas Atkins.

HARTFORD, CONN.
THE CASE, LOCKWOOD & BRAINARD COMPANY.
1883.

TO THE DESCENDANTS

OF THE

EARLY SETTLERS OF MIDDLEFIELD AND LONG HILL,

THIS BOOK

IS

RESPECTFULLY DEDICATED.

1*

PREFACE.

No apology should be necessary in offering to the public any facts of interest hitherto unknown, or in presenting known facts systematized in a convenient manner for reference, yet in the presentation of this little work an explanation, scarcely less than an apology, is needed. More than ten years ago, our beloved father, Thomas Atkins, began collecting historical items and data, concerning Middlefield and Long Hill. Many of these were from personal observation and recollection, and from the stories of the old people, heard in his childhood and held by a memory unusually retentive. By birth he was directly descended from the earliest settlers both of Long Hill and Middlefield, and perhaps no one born within the limits of the town of Middletown ever had more general and intimate knowledge of its history, as handed down by word of mouth from one generation to another. His kinship with nature was so close, his love for her so genuine, that every old or peculiar tree, every stone marked by the ages with uncommon characters, every hidden spring or tangled copse or wildwood growth of shrubs or flowers in the wide vicinity were his own acquaintance. It was his delight to go "across lots" to any place, especially with some young companions, to whom he could point out his loved objects, and with whom he could climb to the tops of the hills and catch the distant views. No hilltop near but had borne the impress of his feet in childhood and in old age, even to beyond fourscore. It is true to say he "possessed the land," that superior possession not limited by legal terms but bounded only by the shifting horizon. This "History" was a cherished work of his, and for ten or twelve years he was putting MS. with MS. with the expectation of sometime giving them to the public, and some of the later additions were made just before he was called to view the "Sweet fields beyond the swelling flood." We ask the reader to remember, when he observes the incompleteness, or the entire absence of facts or data for which he is searching, that it was the author's intention to have carried out to a more definite detail and enlarged treatment nearly all the subjects touched upon, and we think it true, especially in regard to family records. In compiling these MSS. for the press we have tried to fill in some things attainable to us, but it has been with a groping hand and a continual sense of the lack of that means of linking events with the past which only the far-reaching memory of one who has come in contact with more generations can furnish. Such as these pages are, unfinished or incomplete, we feel that they still possess items

of great value to the decendants of the early settlers of the town of Middletown, and we offer
them with the consideration that in spite of omis-
sions they are valuable for what they do possess,
and that they may serve as a foundation and a
corroboration for some more extensive work
which some future author may build. No one
will ever work in this field of research with a
love for it exceeding his, with more jealous care
for its repute, with more honest pride in the
character of its early people, or with stronger
desire for its prosperous future, or with more
fondness for the "goodly heritage" of hill and
field and dale, which has passed from primeval
beauty to present loveliness under the hands of
seven generations. One has but to attempt to
write the history of any New England village to
be impressed with the fact that he will find her
sons and daughters scattered through the West
and South, and in almost all cases filling positions
of trust and influence in the places of their adop-
tion. Our own town is no exception to this truth.
Her children are scattered far and wide, and
whether in large cities or on the broad prairies
or in the Rocky Mountain Territories, they are
a potent, energetic, and intelligent element in the
population.

We do not deem it inappropriate here to copy
from the obituary notice of our father. Thomas
Atkins was born in Middletown, Conn., March 4,
1797, and died at Port Chester, New York, Jan.

13, 1882. He was the son of Ithamar Atkins, grandson of Thomas Atkins, and great-grandson of Ephraim Atkins, who settled in Middletown in the reign of Queen Anne. He was one of twelve children, six sons and three daughters of whom lived to old age. His mother was Anna Hubbard (daughter of Nehemiah Hubbard). He was born on the morning of the day George Washington went out of office; was married in 1827, and settled with his bride, Lucy Miller (daughter of Jacob Miller and lineal descendant of Thomas Miller the 1st, of Middletown), in the Society of Middlefield, about two miles from his own birthplace in Long Hill. To them were born five children, three of whom are now living. The characteristic of self-dependence was peculiarly strong in him. Nothing that he could do for himself did he wish others to do for him. Even in old age was this apparent. Physically he was a man of rare endowment. He could run, jump, hop, and skip in his old age, and very often, after he was eighty, was he seen playing running games with the children. His health was almost uniform until after he reached fourscore. He laughed at dyspepsia and all kindred ills, and his last sickness seemed untimely, even at his age, for it was produced by a long walk in bad weather—such as a young person would hardly undertake. A violent cold was the result, which developed malarial fever. In character he was gentle and kindly, always ready to render assistance to the helpless and dependent; of strict integrity, and proud of his long line of honest ancestry. In his love of nature, he was as faithful as Thoreau. Not a flower blossomed, or a bird sung, but he knew and welcomed them all. He watched for the first blue-bird as lovingly as the Arctic traveler watches the returning sun, and the fringed gentian of the Autumn woods was sought by him in its native nooks. Of a poetic temperament, the English classics were especially liked, but he found delight in all true poetry. His own hand held "the pen of a ready writer," and many and varied were his contributions to local literature. It would seem fitting to say, for the sake of the young who knew him, that a vast amount of the happiness of his long and happy life came from his pure tastes and the love of nature. We must not forbear to mention his great love for the children. He was called "The Children's Friend." At his own home or wherever he was, they sought him with the quick instinct of attraction.

During a long life of uninterrupted activity, he served with fidelity the interests of society, of government, of law, and education. As a country "Squire" he was often sought to settle the vexed questions arising in all communities. "What is right" was always the standard of settlement. He was a member of the Methodist denomination, and for more than fifty years a regular attendant on divine service. Bound by no

sectarianism, he was at home with all who gath-
ered in his Master's house. From youth to manhood and old age he was a staunch and earnest
advocate of temperance. Born in an age when
temperance as a principle was not widely taught,
he was an example of total abstinence from strong
drink. His Christian serenity and his temperate
life carried into old age much of the joy and
vigor and activity of youth. Life's setting sun
shone full upon his years, and some of his pleas-
antest were spent after he was fourscore.

L. A. D.

HISTORY.

Sowheag, a sachem of Mattabesett, (Middle-town,) gave lands to John Haynes, who was the Governor of the Colonies of Connecticut. This was done before there was any settlement in the town of Middletown, as supposed. About the year 1662, Sepunemo and some other chiefs sold land to Samuel Willis and others, they being agents of the town or settlement. It is thought that the wild lands then lying in the settlement were in the last purchase. Sowheag, as before mentioned, was a powerful chief or sachem. The Piquags of Wethersfield, their Sagamore, Sequin, and others on the east side of the Connecticut river were under him. There were not many wigwams in Middlefield; the country here seems to have been more particularly their hunting ground, for arrow heads and other implements of Indian skill and ingenuity are frequently found here.

MIDDLEFIELD.

The town of Middlefield is four miles long from north to south, and three miles and one hundred and twenty rods wide from east to west, and contains about 8,640 square acres. An actual survey might make it some less. It is bounded. north on Westfield Society, east on

2

Staddle Hill and Long Hill, south on the town of Durham, and west on Wallingford and Meriden.

THE FIRST SETTLEMENT IN MIDDLEFIELD.

The first settlement in Middlefield began about the year 1700. The first settlers were Samuel Allen, Benjamin Miller, and Samuel Wetmore; these persons came from the first society. Soon after this others came and settled in Middlefield: persons by the name of Bacon, Hubbard, Stow, Turner, and Ward; these likewise came from the first society. Soon persons came from other towns. We find the names of Camp, Coe, and Lyman, from Durham; of Birdsey from Stratford; of Bartlett from Guilford; and others by the name of Chilson and Hale.

LOCATION OF THE FIRST SETTLERS.

Benjamin Miller settled in the south part of the town near Coginchaug Swamp, or "Low Meadow," and not far from the West river (Coginchaug). Samuel Allen settled in the north part of the town, on high land, thinking it to be a more healthy location. Samuel Wetmore located himself in the center of the place, nearly opposite the spot where the Methodist Church now stands. A more particular account of the prominent families will be noticed in this work under their proper heads.

THE FACE OF THE COUNTRY.

Middlefield, with the adjacent country, is

beautifully romantic, high ranges of hills running
north and south through its whole extent, with
intervening tracts of level land, and meadows of
surpassing beauty, through which the silvery
waters of the West river wander, nearly its whole
length, blend to form a picture of rare loveliness.

DISTANT VIEWS FROM MOUNTAINS AND HILLS.

The sight from "Coe's Peak," or any of the
high points of Besek or of the Western Hills, is
grand and enchanting to the observer. Britain
at the north, with its tall spires pointing heaven-
ward, and its city buildings, seems to repose in
quiet in a lovely valley. Cromwell and Portland
in the northeast present charming scenery. The
deep excavations in brown stone on the banks
of the River Connecticut, look like some old
frowning castle wall with its lofty battlements,
and Cobalt Mt. sits like a fair nymph bathing
her feet in the soft waters of the Connecticut.
Durham at the south, with its glittering spires,
seems to rest in a sheltered vale, as in a sacred
spot, where no unhallowed foot dare intrude.
Hills and dark crested mountains surround it on
almost every side. Wallingford at the west,
with its fenced farms, looks like a pleasure
garden.

MIDDLEFIELD FALLS.

The Middlefield Falls near the northeast
are one of the most lovely cascades in nature.
Here the water tumbles down the flinty rocks a
distance of thirty-five feet, and the sight is grand
at freshet time. Here the geologist may take

lessons, the scientist contemplate the beauty and majesty of this wonderful creation, the poet catch the fire of inspiration and tune his songs to heavenly music, and the divine see traces of the fingers of Deity and be led to exclaim, "Great and marvelous are thy works, Lord of earth and heaven!"

LITTLE FALLS.

In the eastern part of Middlefield are the "Little Falls," a lovely sight, where the water falls down the slaty rocks, step by step, near one hundred feet, and then flows into the powder mill pond. A visit to this lone and silent place will well pay the lover of solitude or any one fond of wild and romantic scenery.

SAW MILL HOLLOW,

Lies a little south of the Middletown City reservoir. Here is wild and lovely scenery, the gentle cascades and old primeval trees with arching, tangled boughs that overhang the stream are food for thought. Here fossil fishes are found, in this "Hollow," some of them quite perfect.

RIVERS, BROOKS, AND SPRINGS.

The West river was so called from its being west of the City of Middletown. Its Indian name was Coginchaug. The main branch of this river starts from a spring at the base of Totoket Mt. in North Guilford, and running northward unites with two other streams of note in Durham meadows, or (Coginchaug Swamp). Its course from the meadows of Durham is northwardly, bearing toward northeast as it enters Middlefield. It receives other tributaries in its meandering course to the Little river, where it unites, in the Boggy meadows, with the Berlin and Newfield branch some half a mile west of the Connecticut river, into which it empties.

WARD SPRING.

Ward Spring, near the head of "Hans" or "Trout Brook," is a noted spring and yields a large supply of water. This spring is a little south of the "Old Burying Ground."

PETER'S SPRING.

Peter's Spring is another noted spring; it is a few rods east of Peter's lane and took its name, as did the lane, from an old slave of one of the Wetmores. Old Peter was freed and had a small house near this spring; this was more than one hundred years ago; scarce any trace of the freedman's hut now remains.

CRANK SPRING.

Crank Spring, which is noted for its clear cold water, is near the foot of Besek, "Coe's Peak." * It took its name from a certain piece of land called the "Crank," bounded partly on Durham and partly on Wallingford line. The lot received its name of crank from the shape of the

* This explanation was obtained through the Lyman family, and seems plausible.

2*

lot on the southwestern side, which is that of a crank, thus:

Durham.

——————| Wallingford.

Middletown.

DARROW BROOK.

Darrow Brook took its name from Nicholas Darrow, because it wandered much of its way through his land, until its unison with the West river.

LITTLE FALLS BROOK.

The Little Falls Brook rises in the east school district, and runs northwardly till it unites with the West river at the Powder Mill Pond. The "Falls" are just above the entrance to the pond.

HANS' BROOK.

Hans' Brook took its name from a man by the name of Hans, who had a house and barn on the lot north of Hans' bridge.

POWDER HILL.

Powder Hill, in the southwest part of Middlefield, is the highest cultivated land in the town, and higher than any in the old parent town of Middletown. It is over five hundred feet above the tide water of the Connecticut river. What gave this hill its name is not exactly known, unless we accept the tradition of the Indian who lost his powder-horn on this hill and spent much time in searching for it; but there is another theory that deserves consideration, which is, that it obtained its name from the soil, and a dark sand that is lodged in the crevices of the rocks, resembling powder. There is a valley between Powder Hill and Besek Mt. where is a very cold spring of water that issues out of the rocks. This spring is called Crank Spring, it is here under the large maple, that parties who visit Coe's Peak leave their provisions before they ascend the mountain, and when they become satisfied with the grandeur and beauty of nature, retire to this loved spot to satisfy the inner man also.

CORPORATION.

Middlefield was incorporated in 1744.

CHURCH FORMED IN 1747.

A church of the Congregational order was formed in 1747, comprising nine males and twenty-four females. Rev. Ebenezer Gould was the first minister in Middlefield, after the society was formed in 1747. He was dismissed in 1756. The Rev. Joseph Denison succeeded him in 1756, and died in 1770. Then the Rev. Abner Benedict was ordained in 1771, and in 1785, at his request, he was dismissed. It was said of Mr. Benedict that he was benevolent, and an able divine, and that he used his influence among his people to induce them to free their slaves, the which almost all of them did. In May 1820, Rev. Stephen Hayes was installed joint pastor of Westfield and Middlefield. He was dismissed Aug. 1827; Rev. James Noyes was ordained July, 1827, and dismissed Jan., 1839; Rev. Dwight

Seward supplied the pulpit from 1841 to 1843. Then Rev. A. H. Powell for a short time, 1851; Rev. Willard Jones from 1852 to 1854; Rev. Francis Dyer from 1854 to 1856; Rev. Mr. Lockwood for a short time; Rev. S. D. Jewett from 1858 to 1867; Rev. Theodore Pond from 1867 to 1868; Rev. Andrew C. Denison commenced his labors here, September 1868.

[The early records show that the erection of a "meeting-house"* was one of the first things resolved upon by the early settlers. This was done soon after the formation of the church, and stood where the present Congregational church edifice now stands. At the close of the Revolution and for many years after, religion was at a very low ebb, so much so, that this church became almost extinct. It was re-organized in 1808. Not very long after, the "Conference House" so called, was built to avoid conflict, and to afford a place for worship while the old meeting-house was occupied by Universalists. In 1842 the present church edifice was built, which in 1882 was considerably enlarged and improved.]

* One who well remembers it, thus describes the old "meeting-house." It was a plain building, about as large as the present one before its recent addition. The inside was furnished with high-backed pews with seats all around, and doors. Some were cushioned, some not. The pews were free. There was a seater, who seated the congregation according to age, respectability, and wealth, the higher grades nearer the pulpit. The latter was a high box-like affair with stairs on one side, and overhead a "sounding board" somewhat resembling a round table top a little concave. The gallery was on three sides of the house. The choir sat in the gallery, and the chorister pitched the tunes with the aid of a tuning fork."

CHURCH BUILDINGS.

There are three churches in the town, all standing near the center of the place—Congregational, Methodist, and Episcopal.

METHODIST EPISCOPAL CHURCH.

The first Methodist Episcopal church was built about the year 1829 or 30, and located where the present one stands. The land owned by the Methodist Society was bought of Samuel Birdsey, in part, and Elisha Coe, in part. The original trustees of the Methodist church were, Comfort Hall, Edward Turner, Elias Coe, Elisha Miller, Jr., Marvin Thomas, Isaac W. Baldwin, and Eliphalet Arnold. The deed given by Samuel Birdsey to the trustees, after describing the land says, "To have and to hold the above granted and bargained premises, with the appurtenances thereof unto them, the said Grantees as Trustees, as aforesaid, and to their successors in said office, in trust, for the said Methodist Episcopal church, forever, to them and their own proper use and behoof." In the earlier years of the church the "circuit preacher" ministered to the congregation. For years, at different periods, the pulpit has been supplied from the Wesleyan University at Middletown. The easy distance from the college gave to this church by frequent opportunity, a high order of talent. Some honored names from the list of University preachers have been familiar to this church. Professors

Willett, Lindsay, Newhall, Harrington, Drs. Holdich, True, and others; among the earlier ones were "Father Burrows" and Heman Bangs. For a considerable term of later years, the church has been supplied by regular pastors appointed by Conference. In the year 1866, the old brick church was torn down, and a new and tasteful one built on its site.

EPISCOPAL CHURCH.

The Episcopal church was built in the year 1862. Since its erection its service has been intermittent, the number of people of the denomination in the place being small. Latterly, students from the Berkeley Divinity School, Middletown, have officiated there.

UNION SUNDAY-SCHOOL CHAPEL.

The old Falls District school-house, called in times past the "Bell school-house" was moved from its site when the new school-house of that district was built, and placed a little farther east, on land owned by Thomas Atkins. It was refitted and converted into a chapel for the use of a Union Sunday-school, and for Union religious service on Sunday evenings. The Sunday-school has been sustained from its organization in July, 1877.

SCHOOL BUILDINGS.

Middlefield is divided into four school districts. The North, East, South, and Falls districts. It has four school-houses. Each district has a school house located near its center, and all the school buildings are in modern style and in good condition (1880).

POPULATION IN 1815.

Number of families, 92. Of these 41 were Congregationalist; Universalist, 36; Methodist, 6; Baptist, 5; Episcopalian, 1. (This classification we find in "Dr. D. D. Field's Statistics," which we think needs correction.) The population was about 450.

LANDS DONATED FOR SCHOOL PURPOSES.

There were lands donated for school purposes, upon the hill south of the wringer manufactories. The farm of Elihu Stow was a part of the land donated, and when the commissioners sold the land the buyers supposed that it would be free from taxes. Bela Coe purchased the old Stow place. He claimed exemption from taxes, as some others did owning school lands. This was in 1826. Captain Bela Coe rated 104 acres of school land. The writer of this history was then assessor of the third district of Middletown, and found no law that would exempt school lands from taxation.

SCHOOLS.

[Those who studied geography in the common schools of New England forty or fifty years ago learned that Connecticut was "famed for her common schools." This was a just tribute, but it was a comparative one. Education, according to the standard of what was required to be taught in the schools of that day, was carefully attended to, and provision made for its support. Fifty or sixty years ago but few branches were taught. Arithmetic (Daboll's), geography, reading, spelling, and writing compassed all. Language lessons, or the grammar of any language, were hardly included. It must be said for this department, so lacking at that day, that the reading books used in the schools were usually compiled from the best English writers—Pope, Addison, Shakespeare, Goldsmith, Sterne, and others. No modern readers furnish purer or richer examples of thought, style, and construction. Daboll's arithmetic, although not followed by algebra or the higher mathematics, was mastered by the farmer boys in the school-room, or before the blazing fire in the great old-fashioned kitchen on winter evenings, perhaps aided by the teacher who was " boarding round," and the same discipline of mind attained as if grappling with higher propositions under more liberal conditions. Geography, for want of explorations, and means to communicate knowledge of the earth's surface, was often faulty. An old geography of this time, picked up from some garret collection of stowed-away books, would make a school boy of the present day laugh. America, Africa, parts of Europe, Asia, and the Isles of the Sea would hardly be recognized except by general outline. Internally a large portion was unknown or misunderstood. Penmanship in the schools of sixty years ago was not at the same discount. The old-fashioned quill pen, if made by an adept, was a better pen than the ordinary steel one used in schools now, and if any one doubts whether the chirography of that day compares favorably with this, let him search out the old manuscripts or the old writing-books of the best writers of that time. The uniformity, legibility, and beauty of the hand-writing of our fathers and grandfathers compel our admiration. Such penmanship would bring a light to the face of any editor of the present day, accustomed to decipher the hieroglyphics of modern authors. A teacher of the "old school" time remarked in our hearing that he used to make and mend forty quill pens for his school. Of his sixty scholars, forty were writers. The schools of Middlefield, until within the last thirty or forty years, were of the same order as those of the State generally. Of the older families of Middlefield there were those who were always warmly interested in its schools; the Augurs, Lymans, Stows, some of the Coes, and others. Warren P. Stow was very earnest in the cause of education. The old-time "Examining Committee" used to take pride in not letting a candidate for teaching slip through too easily. More than once a student from the University of Middletown has been sent sorrowfully away, not able

3

to pass the examination by the Middlefield school committee. The examining committee used to visit the schools and watch the progress with great interest. Many still remember the visits of Mr. Marvin Thomas, accompanied by his wife, who, with her knitting, would sit and calmly review the school, apparently with real enjoyment. A higher standard has prevailed in the schools since thirty or forty years ago. Formerly the teachers were young women in summer and young men in winter, thereby necessitating a disadvantage by repeated change of the manner of instruction. Now teachers remain term after term, and are very generally drilled in the normal schools. The standard and range of studies compare favorably with other places of the same size in the State.]

FACTORIES AND MILLS ON THE WEST RIVER.
GRIST MILL.

In the early settlement of Middlefield, William Miller built a grist-mill at the Falls, where the cotton factory now stands. (William Miller was born in Middlefield and married a daughter of Ambrose Clark of Long Hill, "Lord Am."—as he was called.) Most of his children were born at the Clark house in Long Hill. He moved back to Middlefield about the year 1755. The mill ceased grinding about the year 1800, for the mill was old and worn, and the miller was old and infirm, and ceased work. A saw-mill took the place of the old grist-mill, built by Joshua Stow and Jacob Miller, son of William.

Jacob Miller had a fulling mill under the saw-mill, he being a cloth dresser. His shop for dressing cloth stood on the south bank of the river, just over the bridge, and near or over a rivulet, which was handy for dyeing and rinsing cloth. Willard Miller, son of Jacob, carried on the cloth-dressing business several years after his father gave it up. The saw-mill was not profitable to the owners, and sawing ceased about the year 1808. Richard M. Bailey repaired and fitted up the old saw-mill, and run it to profit for several years for a considerable time after the cotton factory was built, using the surplus water.

The cotton factory was built by the Falls Manufacturing Company in 1847. Some years after an addition was made to the original building. In 1874 the factory was burned, with all the machinery, and in 1874 a new company was formed, called the Russell Manufacturing Company, and a new building was erected, much larger than the old and with more ample means for spinning cotton yarn. This building is nearly two hundred feet long and thirty-eight feet wide, and has a wing. A part of the main building is five stories high. At this factory is spun each week four thousand pounds or more of fine double and twisted yarn, and so perfect is the machinery that only fifty-two hands are necessary to do this great amount of work— twenty-eight girls and twenty-four men and boys.

SNUFF MILL.

There was a mill erected near the "Falls" about the year 1779 or '80 by a Mr. Shaler of the city of Middletown, for the manufacture of snuff. This mill stood a few yards northwest of the saw-mill. The water was taken from the "Falls" and carried to an overshot wheel in a trough. This mill ceased running in a year or two, the manufacture of snuff not being very profitable. Subsequently, and after being idle some years, the mill was repaired and fitted up for the making of buttons. After running about two years, the building took fire and the machinery, stock, and all were destroyed by the fire, which happened in the dead of night.

POWDER-MILL.

There was a small powder-mill located on the west side of the river, about fifteen rods north of the Falls. The water was carried in a trough, across the gulf and emptied into a ditch, along which it ran several rods, and then was conducted on to a small overshot wheel. A man by the name of Curtis owned and operated this mill. He lived in Durham; the mill blew up Feb. 18, 1806; Curtis was blown across the river; he was found wallowing in the snow dreadfully burned; he lived but a short time after he was found. He used to leave the mill in operation nights, and go home to Durham, and sometimes he was not back until late in the morning. Two boys were in bathing one Sunday morning, when they discovered the powder-mill to be on fire; they went and put the fire out, carrying water in their hats. The gudgeon, for the want of lubrication, had got so hot as to set the wood that came in contact with the iron, on fire. These two courageous boys were Horace Miller and Benjamin Birdsey.

We will leave the Falls after reverting to the scenery as it was before the death of Hon. J. Stow, he being the owner of this lovely place. The scenery at this time, in the vicinity of the Falls, was wild and secluded; trees had been suffered to grow, and the banks of the river were lined with elms, maples, and dense hemlocks, lending lonely beauty to the spot. The place was visited almost daily during the summer months, by the lovers of nature. To see the Falls and its surroundings was a favorite drive from the city of Middletown.

NAIL FACTORY.

Next below the Falls, a factory was erected by Jehoshaphat Stow, for the purpose of cutting nails. This was in 1798, or about that time. The inventor of the nail-cutting machine was Daniel French of Berlin, Conn. Previous to this

3*

time nails were headed by hand; and here in this obscure place in Middlefield, Conn., were made the first cut nails of iron in the United States, and perhaps in the world. French left Middlefield and went to Cincinnati, Ohio, where he invented apparatus for propelling boats by steam, and the first steam-boat that ascended the Ohio river from Cincinnati was the invention of his genius, and the trial trip was a success. This was in 1816, or about that time.

WIRE WORKS.

Iron wire was made at this nail factory between the years 1812 and 1816, when we were at war with Great Britain. When the war ceased the manufacture of wire at this place ceased, for wire could then be obtained of the English, cheaper than it could be manufactured at home.

WOOL CARDING.

Soon after the close of the wire-making business, the carding of wool was carried on here by J. Casey, for several years, and when carding became unprofitable the business was given up, and for quite a number of years the factory lay idle, and the dam and buildings went to decay. The property was in the right of the heirs of George Casey. In 1845 this mill privilege was purchased and a

PISTOL FACTORY

was erected by a company of young men, namely, Henry Aston, Ira N. Johnson, Sylvester Bailey, John North, Nelson Aston, and Peter Ashton. They took a large contract of the government of the United States for making pistols; an additional contract was granted them. When the work was finished the property was put up at auction by the company, and Ira N. Johnson was the highest bidder, and the property came to him in 1852. Since then, the manufacture of pistols and other things has been carried on by Johnson and others up to the time the factory was burned, which was on the night of the 21st of Sept., 1879. This building was of brick with a stone basement, 80 feet long by 30 feet wide, and two stories high above the basement. Additions to the main building had been made. The dam was built of stone. [By the burning of the pistol factory Mr. Otis Smith, who was at that time doing quite an extensive business there, lost machinery, tools, stock, and goods. Nothing was saved. In Nov., 1880, Mr. Smith again began manufacturing in P. W. Bennett's factory, where he remained until July, 1882. In Dec., 1881, he purchased of Ira N. Johnson, the pistol factory property, and erected thereon a three-story brick building, 100 feet long by 30 feet wide, and is now manufacturing a pistol of his own invention known as the "Smith's revolver;" also several patented articles in the hardware line.]

POWDER-MILL.

Next below on this river is a powder-mill which was established by Vine Starr about the year 1793, and has been in operation most of the time since. There have been several explosions: Hezekiah Clark lost his life when the mill was blown up in March, 1825. This is the only instance directly resulting in death, caused by this mill since it was established, about ninety years ago. Lately there has been a stone dam erected in place of the wood one. This mill is now, and has been for many years, in the hands of the Rand family of Middletown, Conn.

PAPER-MILL.

Farther down the stream there was a paper-mill, built in 1793 by Jehoshaphat Starr and Nehemiah Hubbard. Here paper was manufactured by hand for a number of years. William Coles came from Dorchester, Mass., to Middlefield, soon after the mill was built, and was foreman for twenty-six years, until 1819. Coles and Wright purchased the mill and ran it for some time successfully. Coles bought out Wright in 1824 or thereabout, and continued the business for a short time with profit, when the manufacture of paper by machinery was introduced, and at much less expense than it could be done by hand, and this almost ruined the business at this mill. The proprietor not feeling able to be at the expense of purchasing new machinery for making paper, the business went down. Since then this mill has changed hands several times. Pasteboard and coarse wrapping paper were for a time made here, then squares and bevels by the "Tidgwell Bros," and subsequently the mill property came into the hands of G. W. Miller and P. W. Bennett. This was in the year 1868.

BONE AND SAW-MILL.

Miller and Bennett constructed a "bone and saw-mill" which is still in operation. In 1875, Bennett bought out Miller, and at the present time (1880), in addition to the other business, pistols and machines for cutting washers for wagons and carriages are made here. [Since 1880, besides the sawing of lumber and the manufacture of bone as a fertilizer, an additional business has been started. In Feb., 1882, was begun the manufacture of a patent lathe-tool for the saving of labor in making small tools. Donald D. Smith is the inventor.]

FACTORIES AND MILLS ON THE BESEK RIVER.

This branch of the main or "West river" rises under the brows of Besek mountain, from springs and the commingling of rains and snows. The Indian name of this stream is not known; it is sometimes called Besek because it flows out from Besek mountain. This river wanders and unites with the main river below the Miller bridge.

SAW-MILL.

There was a saw-mill located where the wringer shops now stand, by William Miller, Jr. This saw-mill was built not far from the year 1775. William Miller was killed in his mill November 2, 1795; in the early morning he was found dead near the water wheel. His wife supposed that he had gone down to the "Falls" to see his father, who was sick at that time.

GRIST-MILL.

Further down this Besek stream was a mill where grain was ground. The dam at this mill was built by Elihu Stow. We have no date as to the time—probably near the year 1780. These two mills were the only ones on this stream until, or near to, the time when the reservoir dam was built.

RESERVOIR.

The reservoir dam was built twenty-seven feet high in 1848–9, by those interested in manufactures on this river and on the main river. In the fall of 1852 the dam was raised five feet, and in the fall of 1870 it was raised five feet higher, making the dam thirty-seven feet high. The pond now covers about one hundred and thirty-five acres.

BUTTON FACTORY.

The button shop occupied the first privilege on the Besek stream, and was built in the summer of 1849. The machinery set to running the

6th of August of the same year. A profitable business was carried on here by different companies for years. "Miller, Coe & Bennett" the last company who made buttons here, hired the mill for five years.

WRINGER MANUFACTORIES.

About the year 1820, Ira Bailey and Capt. Alfred Bailey built a distillery, next to the upper bridge on Besek river, and for about ten years Ira Bailey manufactured there New England rum, cider brandy, and a little whisky; the high cost of rye prevented the extensive manufacture of whisky. About 1822 an addition was made to the distillery building, in which wool carding was carried on by Capt. Bailey, and later wood sawing and turning was done there. In 1848, the building was torn down, and in 1849 a new three-story building thirty feet by forty feet was erected on the same site, which was used by Capt. Bailey for a grist-mill, and about two years later it was used by Mark Mildrum & Co., as a machine shop for repair work, and for the manufacture of coal shovels. Next percussion caps were made here by Arnold Watson, who was killed in an adjacent building by an explosion of percussion powder. Britannia ware was also made in the same building, at this time, by Hall & Cotton. Next, wood turning was again introduced, chiefly in the form of match safes, by William W. Bailey, and at the same time and in the same building

John O. Couch made patent iron candle sticks. About 1857, David Lyman, owning the building, manufactured there the "Metropolitan Washing Machine," and later, a clothes wringing machine, and in November 1860 the "Metropolitan Manufacturing Co." was organized as "Metropolitan Washing Machine Co." This company, with extensive additions to the mill from time to time, added steam power, and about 1868 purchased the adjacent mills and water privileges above and below on the same stream, known as the "Button Shop" and the "Bone Mills," and houses were bought and others were built for homes for the workmen employed by this company, in the manufacture of clothes-wringers, washing machines, mangles, etc., of which as many as 15,000 machines per month can be made.

BONE-MILL.

In 1845 Andrew Coe began grinding bone in the old grist-mill, just below where the "Wringer-Shop" now stands. About 1848 he added to the mill, and burnt bone for sugar refining till 1854, when Russell Coe of Meriden bought out and carried on the business. Subsequently this mill and privilege were purchased and are now used by the "Metropolitan Washing Machine Co."

BONE AND PHOSPHATE MILL.

Next below on the stream is a "Bone and Phosphate Mill" owned and operated by George

W. Miller. Phosphate and ground bone are made here. The mill was built in 1876.

SAW-MILL.

Just below the last mentioned mill is an old water privilege, now unoccupied. It was formerly used by Horace Skinner for wood-turning and afterward by Roswell Lee for a "Feed and Saw-mill."

GRIST-MILL.

Farther down on the stream a grist-mill was built in 1845. It was in operation from that time till the year 1868, when it was burned. The old overshot-wheel being water-soaked, was not burned, and is still standing.

CARRIAGE SHOP.

Next below is the carriage shop of Isaac H. Cornwell. This shop was built by Albert Skinner in the year 1853 for wood-turning of various kinds. In 1876 it was purchased by I. H. Cornwell, who is now engaged in the carriage-making business.

POLITICAL HISTORY.

Middlefield was a district of the town of Middletown until the year 1866, when, by an act of the Legislature of the State of Connecticut, it was set off as a town.

4

Representatives of the town of Middlefield to the State Legislature:

Moses W. Terrill,	1867
Benjamin W. Coe,	1868
Phineas M. Augur,	1869
Henry Smith,	1870
Peter W. Bennett,	1871
Alvin B. Coe,	1872
Alfred M. Bailey,	1873
James T. Inglis,	1874
Harvey Miller,	1875
John L. Wilbur,	1876
Willis Terrill,	1877
Willis Terrill,	1878
Edwin P. Augur,	1879
Daniel H. Birdsey,	1880
John O. Couch,	1881
Alva B. Coe,	1882
Moses W. Terrill,	1883

BIOGRAPHICAL SKETCHES.

"GOVERNOR" BENJAMIN MILLER.

Benjamin Miller, one of the first three settlers in Middlefield, located himself in the south part, on the east side of Coginchaug or West river, and not far from the Durham line. The country then was wild, the soil unbroken by the white man's hand. Benjamin was a stout, athletic man, and capable of enduring hardships. All settlers in new countries have to endure much, and he was fitted by nature to be a pioneer. Forests were to be cleared, roads made, and bridges built while surrounded by Indians and wild beasts. The first settlers scarcely ever left their homes without taking their guns and dogs. Tradition says the title of "Governor" was conferred upon Benjamin by the early settlers partly because of his influence with the Indians, partly on account of his being a large landholder and of influence in the settlement, and, no doubt, partly because of his character, which appears to have been of a dominant type. It is plain that Benjamin Miller the first was a man of great influence in the early history of Middlefield, both from property and character. The Grand Levy of Middlefield, A. D. 1747, makes him the largest property holder of the whole number of persons (62) subject to the grand levy. Benjamin Miller came from Miller's Farms, or South Farms, in 1700. He was the youngest son of Thomas Miller, who came from Birmingham, England, to Rowley, Mass., and thence to Middletown, Conn. Thomas Miller was one of the early settlers of Middletown. He built the first grist-mill in that town. It stood where one of the manufactories of the Russell Manufacturing Company now stands at the "Farms." Benjamin came with a wife and several small children to settle in the wilds of Middlefield. After the death of his first wife (a Johnson from Woodstock) he married Mercy Bassett from North Haven. In all he had fifteen children—seven by his first wife and eight by his second. From an old record in a Bible in Hezekiah Miller's family is copied the following: "Thomas Miller the first came from Birmingham, County of Worcester, England, and he had five sons and three daughters—first, Thomas; second, Joseph; third, John; fourth, Samuel; fifth, Benjamin."

A list of the names of the children of Benjamin Miller, son of Thomas the first:

Rebecca, the oldest child, married a Robinson of Durham.

Sarah married a Hicox of Durham.

Mary married a Spencer of Haddam.

Benjamin, the oldest son, married Hannah Robinson of Durham.

Hannah married Ephraim Coe of Durham.

Isaac died unmarried.

Mehitable, the seventh child, married a Barnes.

Ichabod married a Stow of Middletown.

Lydia married Eliakim Stow of Middletown.

Amos married Abigail Cornwell of Middletown.

Ebenezer died unmarried.

Martha married Thomas Atkins of Middletown.

Rhoda married Benjamin Bacon of Middletown.

David married Elizabeth Brainerd of Haddam.

Thankful, the fifteenth child, died unmarried.

SAMUEL ALLEN.

Samuel Allen was one of the first three settlers of Middlefield. His house stood on the hill in the north part of the place, nearly opposite the Camp Coe house. It was subsequently owned by Deacon Giles Miller and later by Luman Wetmore. The last of the descendants of Allen were Ephraim and Ichabod, and they left Middlefield more than half a century ago. Once there were in Middlefield four families by the name of Allen—Samuel Allen, Obadiah Allen, Ebenezer Allen, and Widow Margaret Allen.

4*

SAMUEL WETMORE.

Samuel Wetmore settled near the center of Middlefield. The house stood nearly opposite the Methodist church. The well is there to this day, and yields good water. There were nine families by the name of Wetmore in Middlefield in 1747. All owned real estate. Samuel, Daniel, and Caleb were among the first settlers. It is probable that the other families were descendants of these three. Daniel and Caleb settled in the (now-called) Falls school district. Daniel's house stood a little west of the late John Dickenson's house. Deacon Caleb's house stood on the corner now (1881) in possession of Thomas Atkins. The old house was burned down more than eighty years ago and a new one erected in its place. Deacon Caleb Wetmore's daughter married Colonel Halyhigh at the close of the Revolutionary war, and Caleb Wetmore sold out and removed to New York city. Jesse Wetmore, son of Daniel, took down the old one-story house and built the new one. He sold out in 1816 and moved with his family to the state of Ohio.

AMOS MILLER.

Amos Miller, son of "Governor" Benjamin Miller, married Abigail Cornwell. His children were: Ebenezer; Amos, who married Elizabeth Tibbals; Abigail, who married Jesse Coe; Daniel married Elizabeth Hall of Middletown; Elisha married Elizabeth Miller of Middletown ; Joseph unmarried.

ELISHA MILLER.

Elisha Miller was a son of Amos Miller and a grandson of Benjamin Miller the first. Elisha settled on the hill now owned and occupied (1881) by his son, Colonel Amos Miller. Elisha took down the old house and built the present one in its stead in 1795 or thereabouts. He married his cousin, Elizabeth Miller. Their children were : Abel, Abigail, Elizabeth, Jerusha, Mary, Esther, Elisha, Eunice, Ira, George, Amos. Elisha Miller had fine orchards of fruit trees. He was one of the early Methodists, and was a man of sound judgment.

HEZEKIAH MILLER.

Hezekiah Miller was a grandson of Benjamin Miller the first, and settled on the east and west road, north of his grandfather's. (He was the son of David, who was the son of Benjamin the first, who was the youngest son of Thomas Miller, who came from Birmingham, England, about the year 1660 and settled in Middletown, South Farms, or " Millers' Farms," as it was first called.) Hezekiah Miller married Sarah Bassett of New Haven. Their children were : Bradley, Benjamin, Hiram, Harriet, Clara, and two children who died in infancy. After the decease of his first wife he married a sister of hers, and moved to

North Haven, where he spent the remainder of his life.

ISAAC MILLER.

Isaac Miller was a man of note in Middlefield, and was the first one who held the office of justice of the peace in the society. He was the son of Benjamin, who was the oldest son of "Governor" Benjamin Miller. His mother was Hannah Robinson of Durham. Isaac was born February 1, 1738, and married Hannah (daughter of Deacon Joseph Coe,) who was born May 9, 1743.

Their oldest son was Phinehas, who was born January 22, 1764. He was a physician and settled in Georgia. He married Catherine, the widow of General Nathaniel Greene.*

Isaac was born March 21, 1766, and married Irene, daughter of Lieutenant Ichabod Miller. He settled in Paris, N. Y.

Hannah, the eldest daughter, was born August 3, 1768, and was married to Phineas, the oldest son of Mr. Samuel Johnson of Berlin, Conn. There they lived for a time, then moved to Ohio.

Anne was born February 19, 1771, and was married to Obed Stow of Middlefield, son of Mr. Elihu Stow.

---

* It is related that the children of Gen. Greene, being on a visit at "Grandfather Miller's," and having free access to a cellar well stocked with apples, came with their hands full of a certain kind, and said, "Grandpa, *these* are the best apples in the cellar!" This was the beginning of the fame of the favorite "Progress" apple, which went for some time by the name of "Squire Miller's best sort."

Olive was born July, 1773, and was married to Asher, son of Amos Wetmore, Esq., of Whitestown, N. Y.

Ruth was born March 31, 1776, and was married to Elihu, son of Mr. Benjamin Birdsey of Middlefield.

Curtis was born July 9, 1779, and died March 31, 1775.

Samuel was born January 22, 1782, and was married to Mary Gilbert, daughter of Benjamin Gilbert of Newfields.

Lucretia was born July 1, 1784, and married Captain Charles Hubbard of Middletown. He was a sea-captain, and died in the West Indies. Lucretia afterwards married Marvin Thomas of Haddam.

Cornelia was born September 1, 1790, and died March 18, 1795.

Isaac Miller settled a little north of the Abel Birdsey house, the place latterly known as the "Thomas place." He died July 27, 1817, aged 79 years.

CAPT. CHARLES HUBBARD.

Capt. Hubbard married Lucretia, daughter of Isaac Miller, Esq. He was a sea-captain, and died in the West Indies.

The children of Charles and Lucretia Miller Hubbard were, Henry, who died while a student in Wesleyan University.

Isaac, who married in New Hartford, Oneida

Co., N. Y., and removed with his wife and children to California, where he died.

William, who married Mary Mills of Morristown, N. Y., and settled in Indianapolis, Ind., where he still lives, having a family of four daughters and three sons.

Hannah, who married William D. Walcott, Esq., of Whitestown, N. Y. (Mr. Walcott is one of the proprietors of the well known " New York Mills.") They have three sons and three daughters.

LIEUT. ICHABOD MILLER.

Lieut. Ichabod Miller was son of Ichabod the first, who was a son of "Gov." Benjamin Miller (one of the first settlers of Middlefield). Lieut. Ichabod Miller married Elizabeth Bacon of Newfields.

Their children were, Irene, who married Isaac, son of Isaac Miller, Esq.

Rhoda, who married William Babbitt.

Sally, who married Jonathan Turner.

Elizabeth, who died unmarried.

Jesse, who married Susan Wetmore, and after her death, Mrs. Sarah Pryor.

Jeremiah, who married Mary Ives.

ICHABOD MILLER, JR.

Ichabod Miller, Jr., was the son of Lieut. Ichabod Miller, and through father and grandfather, a direct descendant of Benjamin, the first. He was born Jan. 25, 1771, and married Sarah

E. Birdsey, who was born Jan. 18, 1776. He lived in the north district of Middlefield not far from where the North School House now stands. He was a vigorous, active man, and a constant worker. He was not sparing enough of his physical powers, and died at the age of 58.

The children of Ichabod and Sarah Miller were, Electa, born July 3, 1796.

Martha, born April 15, 1799.

Sarah E., born July 31, 1802.

David B., born March 5, 1805.

Louisa, born Oct. 1, 1807.

Ichabod, born March 13, 1810.

Jesse, born April 17, 1815.

Elbert, born May 20, 1818.

JESSE MILLER.

Jesse Miller was the son of Lieut. Ichabod Miller and therefore a great-grandson of Benjamin Miller the first. He married Susan Wetmore.

Their children were, Almon, who married Sarah E. Miller, daughter of Ichabod Miller.

Asher, who married Mary Coe.

Charles, who married Emily Cookman.

George, who died unmarried.

Jesse Miller moved, after his marriage, from Middlefield to Turin, N. Y.

ALMON MILLER.

Almon Miller, son of Jesse Miller (who was the son of Lieut. Ichabod Miller) married Sarah E. Miller. The following is from an obituary notice published in the "Middletown *Constitution*" of Jan. 9, 1883:

"Almon Miller was born in Turin, New York, Aug. 30, 1802, and died in Middlefield, Dec. 31, 1882. He was well known in the city of New York, having been in active business there for twenty years, meeting with success, and also the reverses incident to business men ; yet never, in prosperity or adversity, did he lose his good name for honesty and integrity, which characterized his large business transactions. Benevolent and charitable in disposition, always ready to help the poor and friendless, many a poor child and orphan have found a shelter beneath his hospitable roof. He will long be remembered by those who were the recipients of his bounty in their early days."

GILES MILLER.

Dea. Giles Miller settled in the north part of Middlefield. Though not one of the earliest settlers, yet being a prominent man, he deserves an honorable place in this history. He was a descendant of Thomas Miller the first, through his son Joseph, brother of Benjamin ("Gov." Miller). Thomas Miller, the first, came from Massachusetts to Middletown, and settled in South Farms, soon after the settlement of Middletown. Dea. Giles Miller and family were of the Congregational order, and exerted a strong religious influence in the community. This tribute to their character is paid by one of their descendants. " Puritans, with all that the name implies, whether good or bad, in politics or faith. So far as I know, or have ever heard, no stain ever rested on the name or character of any of them. This, with the sterling qualities that belonged to the Puritans of that day, is the only inheritance of which their descendants can have any title to be proud, and the only thing of which I take pleasure in saying that I am proud."

The children of Dea. Giles Miller were,

Asher.

Phineas.

Giles.

Thankful, wife of Prosper Augur.

Elizabeth, wife of Col. Elisha Coe.

ASHER MILLER.

Asher Miller, son of Dea. Giles Miller, removed from Middlefield to the city of Middletown. He was Mayor of the city, Judge of Probate, and Representative in the General Assembly of the State of Connecticut. All these offices of trust he filled to the acceptance of the people. The following is copied from "Fields' Centennial Address : "

" Asher Miller, a native of the Parish of Middlefield, belonged to a class in Yale College which was graduated in 1778, and has always been admired for the amount of talent it contained. He ranked well in his class, and after he

5

left college made himself acquainted with geology, mineralogy, and chemistry, much beyond scholars generally, at that time. He became a lawyer, and the people here esteemed and honored him. Though it is not likely that he began to practice law before 1780, yet in 1785 he was elected a Representative to the Legislature, and repeatedly afterward; and the Legislature so esteemed him for his knowledge of law and his integrity, that in 1793 they appointed him a Judge of the Superior Court. He resigned his seat in 1795. Sometime after, he went to the South to survey a tract of wild land about the mouth of the Yazoo River, for a company who were hoping out of that land to realize a fortune. He was again elected to the Legislature, was long an assistant, and for many years presiding Judge of the County Court and of Probate.

GILES MILLER.

Giles Miller, son of Dea. Giles Miller, left Middlefield and went to Westmoreland, N. Y., leaving his son Giles in Middlefield, a settler in the part now called Falls District. His son Abner went with him to Westmoreland. A grandchild says: "My two grandfathers were zealous on the side of the Colonies in the contest for independence. My grandfather Giles, as I have always heard, was a soldier in the army, under Washington, and was in the engagements on Long Island and around the city of New York."

Giles Miller married Jennie Malcolm, who was of Scotch descent. Their children were Abner, Asher, Giles, Edmund, Eunice, and Harriet.

GILES MILLER.

Giles Miller, son of Giles Miller and grandson of Dea. Giles Miller, settled in that part of Middlefield now called Falls District. He married Clarissa Miller, daughter of William Miller, Jr. Their children were :

Lewis,	Maria,
Frederick,	Ellsworth,
Asher,	Oliver,
Emily,	Franklin.

WILLIAM MILLER.

In the early years of Middlefield, William Miller, born in Middlefield and son of James and Rachel Tryon Miller, and grandson of Thomas Miller (who was brother of "Gov." Benjamin), married a daughter of Ambrose Clark of Long Hill. (Ambrose Clark was one of the earliest settlers of Long Hill, and was called "Lord Am," on account of his being so great a land holder.) William Miller occupied, for a time, the homestead of Ambrose Clark, and most of his children were born at the Clark house. He sold out the homestead to Ithamar Atkins, removed back to Middlefield, and built a gristmill at the "Falls," where the cotton factory now stands, about the year 1775. The mill ceased grinding about the year 1800.

JACOB MILLER.

Jacob Miller, son of William Miller, was born in 1744 (the record says "most of the children of William Miller were born at the homestead of his father-in-law, Ambrose Clark of Long Hill"). Jacob Miller and Joshua Stow built a saw-mill in the place of the old grist-mill of William Miller. Jacob Miller had also a fulling mill under the saw-mill, he being a cloth dresser. His shop, for dressing cloth, stood on the south bank of the West river, just over the bridge near the falls, and near a rivulet which was handy for dyeing and rinsing cloth. He was a man of great vigor and activity. A grandchild of his well remembers his running after his cows at the age of 82. He lived to the advanced age of 92. He never had a physician until he was over 70. If he was sick he would take no medicine, but would go without eating until he got well. He married Mary Crowell of Long Hill. He has been heard to remark that he "drew a prize when he got Mary Crowell."

The children of Jacob Miller and Mary Crowell Miller were:

Jacob, who married Ruth Camp, daughter of Luke Camp and grand-daughter of David Coe.

Horace, who married Harriet Barnes.

Sally, who married Reuben Hall of Wallingford.

Eunice, who married Noel Ives.

Mary (Polly), who married Jacob Atkins of Long Hill.

John Willard, who married, first, Betsey Ives; second, Mrs. Polly Miller.

JACOB MILLER, Jr.

Jacob Miller, son of Jacob Miller, was born in Middlefield in 1781. He married Ruth Camp (daughter of Luke and Grace Coe Camp, and grand-daughter of David and Hannah Coe of Middlefield). Jacob Miller settled in the Falls District, not far from his father's home, on property once owned by Dea. Caleb Wetmore, one of the early settlers in Middlefield. The old house occupied by Caleb Wetmore was burned down eighty or ninety years ago, and a new one erected in its place. (About fifty years ago, Thomas Atkins, who married the daughter of Jacob Miller, Jr., refashioned the house and built a new barn on the premises.) Jacob Miller, though inheriting a strong and enduring constitution from his parents, died at the age of 35 from exposure to cold after the measles had begun to develop in his system. Considering the measles not worth minding, he went about his employment, which was that day one of peculiar exposure.

The children of Jacob and Ruth Miller were:

Lucy, who married Thomas Atkins of Long Hill.

5*

Asher, who married Sarah Cornwell of New-fields.

HORACE MILLER.

Horace Miller, second son of Jacob Miller, married Harriet Barnes, and settled at the homestead of his father. He died in the prime and vigor of manhood, at the age of 37, of epidemic typhoid, in the year 1825. The year 1825 was called the "sickly year" in Middlefield. Seventeen persons, all in the strength of man and womanhood, were swept down by typhus fever. One who lived at that day says that for a long distance, extending through a considerable of the northeastern part of Middlefield, there was one sick in almost every house. It is noteworthy that the fever succeeded a season of excessive drought.

Horace Miller left his wife with six children, the eldest not 13, the youngest an infant. The following in regard to this mother is quoted from the pen of one of her daughters: "My mother was a very energetic woman. She was obliged to manage the farm, and attend to all her other duties. I well remember her going 1½ miles to feed and take care of the cattle, when it was so cold and stormy that her clothes were frozen stiff upon her. She was always cheerful and happy, and left no stone unturned to make others happy. She was very active until the last of her life. She was 83 when she passed away, and the summer previous she was spending a few days with her children on Long Island, where they had a party of young people, and she danced with one of her grand-children."

The children of Horace Miller and Harriet Barnes Miller were:

Augustus, who married Lavinia Bristol and moved to Ohio.

Horace, who married Laura Hale, grand-daughter of Joshua Stow.

Harriet A., who married Charles R. Miller and moved to Ohio, afterward to East New York.

Mary, who married Morris C. Burch of New York City.

Jacob, who married Mrs. Elizabeth Robinson (before her first marriage, Elizabeth Soloman).

JOHN WILLARD MILLER.

John Willard, youngest son of Jacob Miller, settled near his father, and carried on the cloth-dressing business several years after his father gave it up. He married Betsey Ives, who died of typhus fever in the year 1825.

The children of J. Willard and Betsey Ives Miller were:

Charles, who married —— Rich of Durham.

Harvey, (Capt.)

Maria, who married Henry Miller of Middlefield.

For his second wife, J. Willard Miller married Mrs. Polly Miller. Of this union there was one child, Louisa.

TALCOT.

The Talcots were early settlers in Middlefield. They bought the most eastern section of land lying in the parish; it joined the Bacons' section in Long Hill. The Talcots sold out long ago and moved to the Black River country, N. Y. In 1747, we find the names of John Talcot and Hezekiah Talcot, land-holders.

RICE.

Hezekiah Rice bought the house and farm of the Talcots; he married Lydia Stow and settled there. Their children were Betsey, Harriet, and Martina; he sold his home farm to Samuel Birdsey, and built a house west, on a corner lot, not far from half a mile from his old residence. Subsequently, he sold his place to his son-in-law George R. Miller, and moved to Meriden.

CHILSON.

John Chilson was an early settler in Middlefield; he owned land in the South School District, on the hill. There is land now called Chilson land. John Chilson died in 1747; Asaph Chilson's wife died Sept. 5, 1761; Hope Chilson was the last of the Chilsons. It is supposed the rest moved away. Hope Chilson died Nov. 3, 1803.

CAMP.

Abraham Camp, and Edward Camp, were early settlers in Middlefield; they came from

Durham. Edward Camp had a freehold estate in 1747, £86, 1s.; Abraham Camp £63, 12s. Edward Camp's house stood near the brook, on the main road, near where stands the "Turning Shop." There were two Camp houses in the East School District; one, the Fairchild Camp house, owned by Dennis Coe (a new one erected in its place in 18—). Fairchild Camp sold out and moved to Durham. The other Camp house is owned by the "Russell Manufacturing Company," and is quite an old house. The Camps have all faded out of Middlefield, and no one of the honored name of these ancient families is left.

HUBBARD.

Ebenezer Hubbard was an early settler in Middlefield; his house was in the North School District; his property in 1747 was rated at £64, 6s. He was a descendant of — Hubbard, one of the early settlers in Middletown. There were several other families by the name of Hubbard in Middlefield; Elijah Hubbard* and Jedediah Hubbard, these last-named perhaps children of Ebenezer the 1st. These early settlers are all gone. Submit Hubbard was the last; she died March 2, 1825, aged 83 years.

HALE.

Hezekiah Hale, though not among the earliest settlers, was a prominent man in the Society. His house stood on Jackson Hill, nearly opposite the Joseph Coe house. He was sexton for many years (see in the table his record of the dead.)

Hezekiah Hale, oldest child of Hezekiah the 1st and Rachel Hale, was born Oct. 31st, 1778, and married Nancy Miller, born April 6th, 1786. Joseph Hale, son of Hezekiah and Rachel Hale, married Julia, daughter of Joshua Stow.

TURNER.

Stephen Turner was an early settler in Middlefield; he lived in the north school district. He was from the 1st Society; his property in 1747 was set in the Grand Levy at £81, 18s. He died in 1780. There was Jonathan Turner, son of Stephen, and several other families that sprang from Stephen the 1st. Capt. Stephen Turner died Aug. 10, 1804. There were Joel and Jonathan Turner. The name of Turner died out in Middlefield at the decease of Edward Turner.

GUILD.

There were two Guild families in Middlefield in 1747, and still farther back; Jeremiah and Samuel. They had children and relatives buried in the "Old Burying Ground." The Guilds left Middlefield many years ago, and moved to Litchfield county, Connecticut.

HAWLEY.

There were several families by the name of Hawley in Middlefield among the early settlers. Stow Hawley and Samuel Hawley in the North School District, Seth Hawley and Miller Hawley in the East School District. Samuel Hawley died at the age of 66, May 14, 1820, after making quite a display on the new turnpike road

from Middletown to Meriden, and on the corners
in buildings where stood the "toll gate." The
other Hawley families moved away; one to Clinton, and one to Guilford.

DR. JEHIEL HOADLEY.

Jehiel Hoadley of Northford, graduate of Yale
College in 1768, married Hannah Hall of Wallingford, and settled on the "Wm. Birdsey place"
in Middlefield, where he spent his professional
life. He made a specialty of colic curing, as
many did in that day. He was one of the original members of the County "Medical Society,"
from which he was dismissed at his request, to
get rid of the taxes. He was called a good doctor in the place. His wife died Jan. 1, 1810, and
he died the following March 2, 1810, aged 66.

BIRDSEY.

John Birdsey, the first, came from England to
Stratford, Fairfield Co., Conn., and from thence
removed to Middlefield. He was an early
settler, but not among the earliest. He purchased a large quantity of wild land. One tract
lay in the southwest part of Middlefield, and the
other tract in the north or northeast part. The
greater part of this last-mentioned tract lay in
Westfield Society. It is said there were 500
acres in this piece. The price paid for this land
was two dollars per acre. It comprised a part
of "Bald's Falls" hill. The land that John

Birdsey and his sons settled upon was the tract first named. This land was bounded east on the center road of Middlefield, and some part of it extended west to the mountain. John Birdsey built a log house on the corner (as the new road would make it), and subsequently he built a two-story framed house, which after his decease was owned and occupied by his son Abel. The house was torn down some years ago. It is related of John Birdsey and his wife that they were very godly people. The Birdseys were a tall, strong race. This anecdote was told by a great-grand-daughter of Benjamin Miller: "One winter, in the early days when the times were pinching and money scarce, John Birdsey bought of his neighbor, Benjamin Miller, a number of bushels of wheat. Not having the money ready to pay for it, he took off his coat and gave that in payment, and wore a woolen frock during the winter." The same lady related this reminiscence of Mrs. John Birdsey, that during this straightened time she went into the woods to gather wool that had chanced to catch on the bushes, to knit an odd stocking for her little boy, who had burned one of his accidentally.

JOHN BIRDSEY, 2D.

John Birdsey, the second, settled a little south of the Lyman house. He married —— Smith of Long Island. Their children were John, Phebe, Ruth, Sally.——

JOHN BIRDSEY, 3D.

John, the third, settled on the homestead of his father. He married Esther Coe.

DAVID BIRDSEY.

Capt. David Birdsey settled on the hill west of the railroad crossing. His children were Sarah, and two children who died in infancy. He lived, seemingly cheerful and happy, on this salubrious and lonely high hill. His first wife died in 1804. He married again, and his second wife died in 1818.

GERSHOM BIRDSEY.

Gershom Birdsey settled a little south of the David Coe place, where the post-office is now kept by the Rev. Mr. Jewett. He married Lucy Coe, daughter of Squire Eli Coe. Their children were Samuel, Gershom 2d, Eunice, Sarah, Charity.— It may be interesting to state that the property of Gershom Birdsey was settled according to the English law, the eldest son inheriting a double portion. Consequently Samuel Birdsey, the eldest, drew a double share. It is said this was the last property settled in Connecticut after this law.

ABEL BIRDSEY.

Abel Birdsey settled on the old homestead of his father, John, the first. His children were William, Seth.—His wife died in December, 1791. He married a second wife by the name of Skinner, who died in 1846.

6

BENJAMIN BIRDSEY.

Benjamin Birdsey settled not far from the Middlefield Falls. His house stood a little back of the house now occupied by Lewis Miller, and was burned down in 18—. He married twice. His first wife was a Hall, from Wallingford. Their children were Elihu, and a child who died in infancy. His second wife was a Meriam. Their children were John, Elisha, Benjamin, Lucy, and Abigail.

OLD POMP.

Old Pomp, a slave of John Birdsey, was left in the care of Abel Birdsey. He died in 1831. He was blind and quite old when he died. He was the last of the slaves in Middletown. After he was old and blind, he was once found building his fire with the back-log against the closet door, thinking it to be the fire-place. It was discovered in time to save him and the house. Old Pomp was a well-known and appreciated character in his day.

FREEMAN.

David Freeman, rather an eccentric man, died in 1826. He lived several years in an old Wetmore house, where now stands the Methodist parsonage. He had a collection of many odd and curious things. He spent his last days in Uri Coe's house on Powder Hill.

PARSONS.

The Parsons were early settlers in Middlefield. They lived in the East School District. In the

list of 1747 are found the names of Aaron Parsons, Moses Parsons, Simeon Parsons, Ithamar
Parsons, and Timothy Parsons, all landholders.
No one in the district is now known by the
name. All gone, long ago.

JOHN LYMAN.

John Lyman was an early settler in Middlefield. He came from Durham in 1741, and
settled on the farm which is now in the Lyman
family. This farm has been in the possession of
the family for about a hundred and twenty-four
years. It was purchased (in part) in 1741 by
John Lyman, then 24 years old, of Ephraim Coe
of Middlefield (afterward of Durham), who, in the
deed describing one of the pieces of land, says,
"lately bought of Benjamin Miller." (Ephraim
Coe married Hannah, a daughter of Benjamin
("Gov.") Miller.) It is undetermined who was
the builder of the first Lyman house. It was a
"lean-to house," and stood eight or ten rods south-
east of the present home. "Thomas, the grandfather of John, was born in Windsor, Conn., about
1649, removed to Northampton, Mass., and thence
to Durham, between 1708 and 1715. Richard,
the grandfather of Thomas, was born in High
Ongar, England, twenty-five miles northeast of
London, in 1580, and arrived in Boston, with his
wife and five children, Nov. 4, 1631, in the
ship 'Lyon,' in which came also the Rev. John
Eliot, 'Apostle to the Indians;' also the wife of
Governor Winthrop, his eldest son, and wife, and

other families, in all about sixty persons. They were ten weeks at sea. Richard Lyman lived first in Charlestown and Roxbury; joined the church of Eliot in Roxbury, and in 1635 came with a party of about a hundred, through the woods, in fourteen days, to Hartford, where he died in 1640."

DAVID LYMAN.

David Lyman, son of John Lyman, succeeded him, and settled on the homestead. He was colonel of a regiment of cavalry in 1810, or near that time. He took down the old house and built a new one on the same site. He died in 1815.

WILLIAM LYMAN.

William Lyman, son of David Lyman and grandson of John Lyman, settled on the homestead of David his father. He was born Aug. 21, 1783, and died of pneumonia Jan. 28, 1869. He was one of those who formed the Congregational Church in Middlefield in 1808, and was always one of its pillars. In the temperance movement he early took a decided stand, giving up the use of all intoxicating drinks, and banishing from his hospitable home the custom of offering even wine and cider to guests. When he told his mother, whose home was in his family, that he had decided upon this step, she with great astonishment in her manner said, "Why William! not when Mr. Watkinson and Uncle Micah come?" The Congregational parsonage was probably the first building raised in Middlefield, without rum (1831 or '32). Good men in the church pleaded with tears for the old custom, and when they found that Mr. Lyman was immovable in his purpose, so many went home grieved, angry, disgusted, that the raising could not be finished that day. In the anti-slavery contest he was no less earnest and enthusiastic, and ready, ever, to speak and act as his conscience dictated, though by doing so he often incurred the censure of even good men, and became as unpopular as other Abolitionists. As a neighbor and in his family, he was kind, tender, and generous. Ever ready to submit to inconvenience for the sake of others, he was a gentleman of the old school; a school which no modern manners have ever excelled in courtly politeness or genuine courtesy. He was a cousin of Dr. Lyman Beecher, both being grandsons of John Lyman, the 1st of the Middlefield Lymans.

His wife was Alma Coe, daughter of Col. Elisha Coe. She was, like her husband, of strong mind and excellent character. She died in 1875, in her ninetieth year. Great age has been common in Middlefield. Their children were:

Phineas.

Adeline.

Elizabeth, who married Rev. Chas. L. Mills.

David, who married Catherine Hart.

Sarah, who married Rev. James T. Dickinson.

Elihu.

Adeline Urania.

6*

DAVID LYMAN.

David Lyman, son of William Lyman, settled
at the homestead of his father. He was born in
Middlefield, Oct. 19, 1820, and married Catherine
E. Hart of Guilford, Conn., Jan. 30, 1849. He
died at his home in Middlefield, Jan. 24, 1871,
aged 50 years and 3 months. From the numerous obituary notices which appeared in the
journals of Middletown, New Haven, Hartford,
and other places, the following is selected from
the Bennington, Vt., *Free Press*, of Feb. 4, 1871.
" He received a good common school education,
supplemented by a little academical instruction.
At the age of nineteen, he was sent by the
Messrs. Trowbridge of New Haven, to Kentucky,
to purchase mules for them for the West India
market, and by them and the house of ' Alsop
& Chauncey ' of New York, he was kept at
this work for several years. For a short time he
followed it on his own account. At twenty-
seven he was appointed to the trusteeship of a
large estate. In the management of this trust,
which he held up to the time of his death, his
great capacity for business was called into constant requisition. Before long a legal controversy
arose, concerning certain dispositions of the will,
and this controversy ran for ten years through
the courts of Connecticut, and New York, and
the United States Circuit Court. At the end of
this litigation, in which some of the most distinguished lawyers of the land were employed,

Judge Nelson of the United States Supreme Court, in giving a decision of the case at New Haven, said of him, 'His conduct presents a conspicuous instance of great capacity, fidelity, and success, in the discharge of the difficult and responsible duties confided to him by the deceased, under the will; and calls for the commendation of this court. We have rarely known an instance of such faithful, conscientious, and accurate performance of the duties of trustee, and in view of the fact that trust estates are so often, through incompetence or unfaithfulness, wasted, we feel it our duty to give the conduct of this trustee the marked approval of this court.' His chief business for the last ten years of his life was the manufacture of clothes-wringers. For the last four years, however, he had little to do with the active management of this business, his whole time being absorbed—so completely as to shorten his days—by his interest in the New Haven, Middletown & Willimantic R. R., of which he was president. The corporate authorities of the two cities of Middletown and New Haven, as a tribute to his memory, passed, each, a series of resolutions in appreciation of his labors and faithfulness. One of the New Haven resolutions was as follows: 'Resolved, That in the death of David Lyman, the public at large are called upon to deplore the loss of a true man, eminently faithful in the discharge of every duty, attending to every trust committed to his care;

genial, earnest, full of hope, inspiring others with his enthusiasm; who carried to substantial conclusion that great enterprise, the Air Line Railroad, a work of inestimable benefit to this city.'"

PROSPER AUGUR.

Prosper Augur, son Isaac Augur, settled in the northwest part of Middlefield. The following is from his family record:

"1. Robert Augur, who came over to the New Haven Colony, from England, married Mary Gilbert, daughter of Lieut.-Gov. Gilbert, Nov. 20, 1673.

2. His son John, who married Elizabeth Bradley, 1710.

3. His son Isaac, who married Eunice Tyler of Haddam (they having twelve children).

4. Prosper, one of Isaac's sons who settled in Middlefield, and married Thankful, daughter of Dea. Giles Miller."

Their children were,

Elizabeth, who married Comfort Johnson.

Sally, who married Luman Wetmore.

Polly, who was unmarried.

Phineas, an only son, who settled in the neighborhood of his father, and married Esther Kirby, of Upper Houses (now the town of Cromwell).

Prosper Augur was a man of sound mind, self educated; for many years a deacon of the Congregational Church of Middlefield. He was a man of much stability of character, sterling integrity, and great usefulness.

PHINEAS AUGUR.

Phineas Augur, son of Prosper Augur, at the age of sixteen, commenced teaching; at the close of his first examination before Dr. David Dudley Field, of Haddam, the Rector quoted Timothy "Let no man despise thy youth." After teaching very successfully for several years, he died in early manhood, in Nov., 1825, of epidemic typhus fever, which prevailed in Middlefield that season.

PHINEAS M. AUGUR.

Phineas M. Augur, son of Phineas, settled at the home of his father. He married Lucy E. Parmelee of Guilford, Conn.

CAPT. DAVID COE.

David Coe was an early settler in Middlefield. He was the son of Lieut. Joseph Coe of Durham, grandson of John Coe of Stratford, and great-grandson of John the first, son of Robert Coe of England, who came to New England in 1634. *

Robert Coe, the first in America, sailed from Ipswich and probably came from Norfolk, this being the nearest shipping port. He came in the ship "Frances" in the year 1634. His age was 38, that of his wife Ann, 43, his son John, 8, Robert, 7, and Benjamin, 5. He settled in Watertown, Mass., in 1634, where he was made a freeman, Sept. 3d of that year. In 1635 or 6 he removed to Wethersfield, Conn., and thence in

* According to "Burke's Heraldry" all the members of this family of distinction resided in Norfolk Co., England.

1650 to Stamford or Stratford. In 1662 he removed to Hempstead or Jamaica, Long Island, in New York jurisdiction. He was made sheriff in 1669, which office he held until 1672.

His children were,

John, born about 1626, in England.

Robert, born about 1627, in England.

Benjamin, born about 1629, in England.

John, son of Robert and Ann Coe, came to New England in 1634, with his parents, and to Wethersfield, and Stratford, and was of Newtown, Long Island, in 1655, and of Greenwich, Conn., in 1660, and that year was one of the (original) purchasers of Rye, New York. He was Captain, and was appointed a magistrate by Connecticut, and was representative to the "General Court of Connecticut," from Newtown in 1664. He was of Stratford in 1685.

His children were,

John.

Robert.

Jonathan.

Samuel.

David.

John, son of John the first, married in Stratford, Dec. 20, 1682, Mary, daughter of Joseph Hawley of Stratford. His eldest four sons settled in Durham, Conn., where they had families. John died April 19, 1741.

His children were,

Robert, born Sept. 21, 1684.

Joseph, born Feb. 2, 1686.

Hannah, born April 14, 1689.

Mary, born Aug. 11, 1691.

John, born Dec. 5, 1693.

Sarah, born March 26, 1696.

Ephraim, born Dec. 18, 1698.

Catherine, b. Sept. 23, 1700.

Abigail, b. Nov. 11, 1702.

Ebenezer, b. Aug. 18, 1704.*

Capt. David Coe's house stood on the spot where the Rev. Mr. Jewett now keeps the post-office. His son Eli Coe took down the old house and built the present one on its site. David Coe was a brother of Joseph Coe, who settled on the hill north. David Coe married Hannah, daughter of Nathan Camp of Durham (one of the proprietors of the town). She was a zealous christian and an earnest supporter of the Congregational church; sometimes the meetings of that order were held at her house. The religious antagonism of her son-in-law, Joshua Stow, was a great grief to her. She was an economist of the old school. In later life she was known by the familiar cognomen of "Granny Coe." Her character deserves more than a passing mention.

The children of David and Hannah Camp Coe were:

Nathan, b. May 19, 1742.

Jesse, b. Nov. 14, 1743.

* Copied from "History of Torringford, Conn., by Rev. Samuel Orcutt."

Mary, b. Oct. 7, 1745.
David, b. July 21, 1747.
Ezra, b. March 4, 1750.
Hannah, b. Dec. 21, 1751.
Adah, b. July, 1753.
Seth, b. Feb. 20, 1756.
Eli, b. April 11, 1758.
Ruth, b. Oct. 4, 1760.
Grace, b. Oct. 5, 1763.

MARY COE.

Mary Coe, daughter of Capt. David and Hannah Coe, married Daniel Hudson. The following is copied from " History of Torrington, Ct." (Orcutt):

"Daniel Hudson and Mary Coe, his wife, were among the pioneer settlers of the town of Torrington, Litchfield Co., Conn. They came into the parish of Torringford in 1768, and were constituents of that society and church in establishing the pastorate of Rev. Samuel J. Mills, over that people in 1769. As Jacob served Laban seven years for his daughter Rachel to wife, it doth appear that Daniel Hudson served Capt. David Coe for his daughter Mary, for in his will the reading is, " I give and devise to the heirs of my daughter Mary Hudson, £32 18s. The reason why I give them no more is, that my son Hudson had the improvement of my lands eight years, which I judge to be their full proportion to the rest of my daughters." Daniel

Hudson and wife Mary went westward, at that time a tiresome journey, on horseback, and with an ox-cart through the dark wilderness, following a bridle path, and the unmade south road, through the south part of New Hartford, through the northern part of Torringford street, thence to Still River swamp, thence up the mountain gorge to Winchester. On that road they pitched their tent and erected a small one-story house. Subsequently they built a two-story "lean-to" house and became possessed of an extensive farm, the most eligible for tillage and grazing in that region. Here they dwelt, toiled, and prospered, nurtured a family of nine children, seven daughters and two sons, all of whom grew up healthy, industrious, intelligent members of society. The homestead remained in the family ninety-two years, so long as a Hudson remained in Torringford. The household scenes of Daniel Hudson and Mary Coe furnished an instructive horoscope of the future of that family. The active physical and moral energies of the parents, and their numerous daughters and two sons, manifested in the various industries and responsibilities, gave promise of certain success in life. All clad in home-spun and home-made garments, the father and sons in butternut colored or plain, the mother and daughters in plaid or striped short gowns and petticoats, seldom with costly shoes except on extra occasions, offered a scene which society of modern times may feel to despise, but

7

in regard to the prudence and wisdom of which, it might be health to the eyes of many people to see."

The children of Daniel Hudson and Mary Coe were nine daughters and two sons, namely:

Hannah, b. 1767, m. Phineas Elmer.
Rhoda, b. 1768, m. David B.
Molly, b. 1770, m. Z. Wilson.
Grace, b. 1772, m. Ozias Bronson.
Daniel Coe, b. 1774.
Eunice, b. 1776, m. Benjamin Kinsley.
Adah, b. 1778, m. Gen. Uriah Tuttle.
Barzillai, b. 1780.
Clarissa, b. and d. in 1782.
Sarah, b. 1783, d. 1784.
Clarissa, b. 1785, m. Daniel Tuttle.

DANIEL COE HUDSON.

Son of Daniel and Mary Coe Hudson, married Mary, daughter of Capt. Epaphras Loomis, Feb. 16, 1797. She died July 22, 1804. He married 2d, Rhoda, daughter of Noah Fowler. Daniel Coe Hudson died July, 1840, aged 66.

Their children were:

Daniel, b. Mar. 9, 1798, died Mar. 16, 1805.
Erasmus Darwin, b. Dec. 15, 1805.
Daniel Coe, b. Jan. 16, 1808.
Flora Hollister, b. May 6, 1811.
Charlotte L., b. Oct., 1813.
Mary Loomis, b. March 31, 1818.

Dr. Erasmus Darwin Hudson, son of Daniel

Coe and Rhoda Fowler Hudson died at Riverside, Conn., in 1860, aged 75 years. The following obituary notice is copied from the *Medical Register* of New York city for 1881–82, and is an emendation of an obituary notice in the " New York *Tribune* " of Jan. 1, 1881 :

" Dr. Erasmus D. Hudson was born at Torrington, Litchfield Co., Conn., Dec. 15, 1805. His father, Daniel Hudson, was a descendant of Daniel Hudson who landed in Boston in 1630. In 1823 he entered the office of his uncle, Dr. Remus M. Fowler of New Marlboro, Mass., and matriculated subsequently at the Berkshire Medical College, from which he graduated in 1827. The late John P. Batchelder was his preceptor and friend during his college course. During his college vacations he was self-sustaining by teaching school. After graduation he married Martha Turner of New Marlboro, Mass. He settled in practice at Wintonbury and Bloomfield, Conn., and subsequently practiced in Windsor and Torringford, Conn. At Torringford he was the associate and successor of the well known Dr. Samuel Woodward. He was a member of the Berkshire Natural History Society, of the Hartford County Medical Society, Connecticut State Medical Society, and Physician and Surgeon to the Connecticut State Emigrant Hospital. About 1838, he had taken an active part in the temperance reform, and more especially the anti-slavery agitation. He was the general agent of the Connecticut State Anti-Slavery Society until 1842, and subsequently until 1849, of the American Anti-Slavery Society, constantly traveling through the New England, Middle and Western States as a lecturer and organizer of societies and conventions. The intensity of this work in the face of public excitement and constant personal danger, compelled him to retire to private life, although he remained a member and officer of the societies to the time of the Rebellion. In 1850 he engaged in the manufacture of artificial arms and legs at Springfield, Mass., but in 1855 he removed to New York and soon extended his work to a broader field, the treatment by prothetic and mechanical appliances of various forms of physical loss and injury. During and subsequent to the war he applied arms and limbs for the government, but more especially was engaged in adapting apparatus for hip joint and Syme's amputations, and for the cures of resection, paralysis from gunshot injury, etc. He wrote several monographs on amputations and resections, and contributed largely to the reports of the United States Sanitary Commission and the Surgeon-General's Medical History of the War. His services were recognized by an award at the Paris Exposition, 1867, the International Sanitary Society, and the Centennial Exposition, 1876. Throughout, his time and services were always given to the crippled poor gratuitously, and the apparatus supplied to the wounded soldiers was always constructed with a philanthropic zeal, and a thoroughness and conscientiousness which curtailed the usual liberal profits of government patronage. Dr. Hudson was a man of vigorous physique, well preserved by regularity and simplicity of life. He had never been confined a day in bed by sickness, and during 1879 and 1880 had come daily to the city from his country place in Connecticut, a distance of thirty miles. An epidemic of diphtheria caused the death of two favorite grand-children in November, 1880. Dr. Hudson became greatly depressed by this loss, and was seized with pleuro-pneumonia, of which he died at Riverside, Conn., Dec. 31, 1880, aged 75 years and 16 days. His wife survives him. He had three sons, one deceased, and two surviving, Mr. R. F. Hudson and Dr. E. Darwin Hudson, Jr., both of New York city."

JOSEPH COE.

Joseph Coe, the son of Dea. Joseph Coe, and grandson of Lieut. Joseph Coe of Durham, and great-grandson of John Coe of Stratford (grandson of Robert Coe who came from England in 1634), married Elisabeth Cornwell of Westfield, and settled at the old homestead on the Hill.

His children were:

Elihu, b. Aug., 1780.

Millicent, b. March 25, 1782.

Joseph, b. Jan. 31, 1784.

Curtis, b. Jan. 9, 1786.

7*

Lois, b. Jan. 6, 1788.
Esther, b. Jan. 6, 1790.
Enoch, b. Oct. 25, 1791.
Calvin, b. Apr. 11, 1794.
Luther, b. June 1, 1796.
Cyrus, b. May 8, 1798.
Of these children:
Enoch Coe, died Oct. 21, 1798.
Luther Coe, d. Oct. 20, 1798.
Cyrus Coe, d. Sept. 22, 1822.
Joseph Coe died July 9, 1828, aged 76 years, and Elisabeth Coe, his wife, died Jan. 19, 1831. For him was the first grave dug in the new or Central Burying-Ground. He was a man of sound mind, honest in his dealings with men, a rigid Baptist, and somewhat of a theologian.

CAPT. JOSEPH COE.

Joseph Coe married a daughter of William Ward. He removed to South Farms, and while there was made captain of a militia company. He moved back to Middlefield on the Lyman Farm in the East School District. He lived at this place till his father died, then he removed to the old homestead on "Jackson Hill." He represented the town of Middletown in the Legislature of Connecticut, and likewise the Eighteenth District in the State Senate. His children were, Phineas, Osborne, and Ward.

ELIHU COE.

Elihu Coe married a daughter of Eli Coe, Esq. He built a house on the center road, north of the North District School-house, and lived there till the decease of his wife and some time after. She died March 13, 1826. Their children were, Enoch, Luther, and Rachel. He married a second wife by the name of Ward, and removed to Butler's Creek. He lost his second wife, and then removed to the residence of his son-in-law, Isaac Baldwin, in the city of Middletown, where he died, Aug. 24, 1859, aged 78 years.

CURTIS COE.

Curtis Coe was born 1786, and died July 6, 1875, aged 89 years. He married a daughter of the Hon. Joshua Stow, and settled on the Hawley place in the East School District. His wife died in 1834, aged 43. Their children were, Marianne and Cyrus. Mr. Coe had large nurseries of fruit trees, and the fine cherry called the "Coe cherry" was orignated by him. In the latter part of his life he married Sarah Parmelee of Durham.

CALVIN COE.

Calvin Coe married a daughter of Hezekiah Rice and settled in Meriden.

COL. LEVI COE.

Levi Coe was the son of Eli and Rachel Miller Coe, and grandson of David Coe, and was born July 11, 1788. He was the youngest of a family of five children, three sons and two daughters. We copy the following, a just tribute to his character: "His education was such as might be obtained at the practical common schools of his time. The only occupation of his life was farming, in which he was successful, in that he did everything thoroughly, never attempting to do more than could be done well, breaking no more ground than could be well tilled, keeping no more stock than could be well fed. His farming was practical rather than theoretical. He took great pride in the fences, in the crops, and in the stock of his farm. He acquired an enviable reputation in breeding and raising good horses and cattle, the beautiful Devons being his favorite breed, always striving for the best. He was of a hopeful and cheerful disposition, mild and modest in manners, kind and indulgent in his family, considerate and obliging to his neighbors, cautious and conscientious in his transactions, and firm in his convictions of right. His advice was often sought, and his judgment much relied on by others. He filled many offices of trust and responsibility, and always with fidelity, and had the respect and confidence of all who knew him. He was for many years an active member of the State militia, and was advanced to a Colonelcy when military honors were worthy the ambition of any, and when merit alone was the test of such distinction. That he merited the title was attested by its universal application in addressing or speaking

of "Col. Coe." He took a deep interest in the
affairs of his native town, and of the society in
which he lived, and in the church, of which he
was a consistent member. He was also true to
his political party—the Whig party—till it died,
and the Republican party till he died. He was
married to Sarah Ward, daughter of William and
Mary (Miller) Ward, on the 14th of Feb., 1811.
with whom he lived nearly fifty-three years, till
his death, Jan. 16, 1864. His wife survived him
nearly eight years, and died Dec. 10, 1871, aged
84 years. By this marriage there were four
children, to wit :

> Benjamin Ward Coe, born April 28, 1812, who
> married Betsey Birdsey, and died June
> 28, 1877.

> Aurelia Miller Coe, born Oct. 15, 1815, who
> married Ichabod Miller, and died July
> 14, 1873.

> Alvin Bennett Coe, born Feb. 13, 1821, who
> married Harriet Coe, and now (1883) lives
> in Middlefield.

> Levi Elmore Coe, born June 6, 1828, who
> married Sophia Fidelia Hall, and now
> lives in Meriden, Ct.

ELI COE.

Eli Coe, son of Squire Eli Coe, and grandson
of David Coe, married Lois, daughter of Joseph
Coe. Their children were :

Nelson, who m. Phebe Crowell.

Russell, who m. Catherine Birdsey
Esther.
Lewis, who m. Sophia Coe.
Isaac, who m. Sarah Bacon of Westfield.
Eunice, who m. —— Bliss.
Joseph E., who m. Laura Miller.

CAPT. BELA COE.

Capt. Bela Coe lived near the center of Middlefield, in the house built by James Ward 2d, and lately occupied by Cornelius Hall. He married for his first wife Hannah Ward. For his second wife he married Mrs. Ruth Birdsey. Bela Coe was the son of Esquire Eli Coe, and grandson of David Coe. The children of Bela Coe and Hannah Ward Coe were:

Dennis, who married Lucy Birdsey.
William, m. Lucina Cook.
Lucina, m. Roswell Bailey.
Watson, m. Louisa Bacon, of Westfield.
Andrew, m. Caroline Coe, daughter of Calvin Coe.
Rachel, who married Elbert Miller.

Capt. Bela Coe died Oct. 4, 1841, aged 63.

ELIAKIM STOW.

Eliakim Stow, born March 3, 1708, married Lydia Miller (daughter of Benjamin [Gov.] Miller, one of the first settlers of Middlefield). He owned the land from a point east of what is now known as Lee's Mill, west to the top of the mountain, including the Metropolitan W. M. Co's works, etc. He had a flouring-mill, a saw-mill, and afterward a mill for carding wool. His dwelling-house was about fifteen rods southwest of the residence of John O. Couch, Esq. He had seven children :

Eliakim, who died at 23 years of age, and was buried in the old burying-ground, Middle-field.

Sarah, who married and settled in Granville, Mass.

Elihu.

Mary, who married and settled in Granville, Mass.

Dan, who died at the age of 29 years, and was interred in the old ground, Middlefield.

Catherine.

Benjamin, who settled in Granville, Mass.

Catherine married an English gentleman named Hicklyn. After living several years in England, they came to spend some time with her friends in America, and boarded with Joshua Stow. While there Catherine was taken sick and died.

ELIHU STOW.

Elihu Stow, son of Eliakim Stow the 1st, married Jemima Payne, whose parents came from Long Island while the British held possession there, during the Revolutionary war. When they returned at the close of the war, their two daughters, Deborah and Jemima, were left in

Middletown; Deborah, the wife of "Parson Frothingham;" Jemima, of Elihu Stow. Elihu lived in the house with his father, where eight children were born to him. Tradition says, that for this reason,—the house being full of children, and the mother's heart turning to her youngest, her Benjamin, who was childless,—Eliakim and his wife Lydia went to Granville to live with Benjamin, and their remains, after a pilgrimage of more than 90 years, quietly rest in the "Old Graveyard on the Hill," at Granville, Mass.

Elihu's children were:

Elihu, who settled in Granville, where his descendants now live.

Naomi, who married Bela Hubbard.

Joshua, who married Ruth Coe.

Jemima, who married William Kelly.

Obed, who married Anna Miller.

Lydia, who married Hezekiah Rice.

Eunice.

Silas.

Elihu, like the Stows in general, was not afraid to express his opinions, even if in the minority. For instance, he was very much opposed to taxation for the support of the ministry, and refused to pay his tax, allowing his horse to be sold at public auction, rather than act contrary to his convictions. He and his wife withdrew from the church in Middlefield, and united with the "Separatist Church," as it was called, in Middletown, and rode six miles to meeting nearly every

Sabbath. The Stows were generally kind to the poor. One anecdote is told of Elihu. During the general destruction of the wheat crop by the Hessian fly, he was in his field, haying, when a small boy came to have him grind a peck of wheat. He said, "My boy, why didn't you bring more? It will hardly pay to leave my work and start the mill for a peck." "Sir," said the boy, who had ridden six miles to bring it, "Mother would have been as glad to have sent more as any one, but it was *all* she could get." In relating the incident to his wife, he said, "I never went more willingly to start the mill, and took no toll. I found four quarts of wheat and put that in, and wished it was more." His wife was thrown from a carriage and instantly killed, when about 74 years old. He afterward married the widow of a Mr. Wetmore, who survived him. He was buried in the "Old Burying Ground," Middlefield. Of his children, only Joshua, Obed, and Eunice remained in Middlefield. Eunice, youngest daughter of Elihu, was noted for her kindness to the sick, never refusing to go to take care of them, however malignant the disease. She herself was never sick to call a physician, until the time of her death (1838), at about 70 years of age. She died of disease of the heart.

JOSHUA STOW.

Joshua Stow, son of Elihu and Jemima Payne Stow, was born in Middlefield, April 22, 1782,

8

and died Oct. 11, 1842. He married Ruth Coe, daughter of David Coe of Middlefield.

Their children were:

Julia, who married Joseph Hale.

Albert.

Laura, who married Curtis Coe.

Joshua Stow was a man of superior talent, and great force of character. In early life he went, in the employ of the State of Connecticut, to the Western Reserve as a surveyor, and was one of the earliest pioneers in that region. In his first journey, he was carried by Indians from Buffalo to Cleveland in a canoe. He became a very prominent and influential man in his native State (Connecticut), and as a member of the Constitutional Convention of that State, was the author of the Article in the Constitution which secured complete religious toleration, thus placing Connecticut in advance of the times in enlightened legislation.

From another source (that of a niece of Judge Stow,) we gain the following:

"Joshua was a very prominent man in what was known as the Anti-Federalist party, and a warm supporter of the Universalist Church. He enjoyed telling stories, incidents of his boyhood, and none more than his adventures while visiting 'Uncle Ben' at Granville. One day he had been busy all day helping Uncle Ben barrel up flour at the 'Mill,' and having loaded the cart, (a new tip-cart just come into use,) they started for

home up the hill, a mile and a quarter in length.
As they neared the summit, the barrels had
slipped back, or being unused to it, they had not
secured the pin sufficiently, the cart tipped, and
all the barrels went rolling down the hill.
'Uncle Ben' stood without moving a muscle
until the last barrel had ceased to roll, when he
said, 'Josh, if a carpenter came to make me a
new cart, and should even ask me if I'd have a
tip-up-cart, I'd kill him.' The following anecdote will show the persistency of Joshua's character. During the difficulties with the 'Eagle
Bank,' New Haven, three men of Middletown,
Ct., were put under bonds that they would not
leave the city of Middletown. The other two
forfeited their bonds and returned to their business and homes; but Joshua refused to do it, and
for years remained without visiting his home in
Middlefield. His wife would ride in, and con-
sult him in regard to the farm, etc. At last
some interested parties became very anxious to
have him forfeit his bonds. They accordingly
hired a—shall I say—man? to take Mr. Stow
beyond the specified bounds. It was fine sleigh-
ing and he invited Mr. Stow to ride with him.
As they neared the northern limit of the city,
Mr. Stow said, 'You must stop, I cannot go
farther.' 'Never mind,' said the *man*, and struck
his horse a sharp blow. 'But I *do* mind,' said
Mr. Stow, and rolled from the sleigh before the
limit was reached. His mind remained good to

an advanced age. He was confined to the house with a severe cold, but no alarm was felt until they found him dying."

The following obituary from a western paper has been preserved by a great-grandson of Judge Stow:

"Died at his residence in Middlefield, Conn., on the 11th of Oct. (1842), Hon. Joshua Stow, in the 81st year of his age. Truly, 'a good man has fallen in Israel.' His name has since 1799 been associated with the history of the Western Reserve, and no man has contributed more to its advancement and prosperity. He visited this country in 1799 as agent for the Conn. Western Land Company, having charge of the surveying party which was sent out by the company that year, to survey the "Reserve" into townships. They landed at Conneaut harbor, on the 4th of July of that year, and there celebrated in that 'temple not made with hands,' the glorious anniversary of our Independence. This commenced the settlement of the Reserve. It was the first step in the march of improvement which has made 'this wilderness to blossom like the rose.' Since that time his name has been closely identified with the improvement and settlement of the Reserve. It is a fact, perhaps not generally known, that of the whole number of individuals composing the Conn. Western Reserve Land Company (and most of them were wealthy), but few saved themselves by the investment. Mr. Stow has largely contributed to the prosperity of this town. He has made liberal investments of capital in erecting extensive mills upon his water-power, which are now standing. We believe Judge Stow was the last surviving member of the 'Conn. Western Reserve Land Company.' Judge Stow has filled important offices in his own State with great credit to himself. He was for several years chief judge of the county court, for several years a member of both branches of the Legislature, and for more than twenty years he filled the office of Postmaster at Middletown, Conn. This last office he held until within two years of his death, when he resigned, on account of the increasing infirmities of old age. As a member of the Legislature and judge, he gained the reputation of a wise, sagacious, and honest man. He was a soldier of the Revolution, and received from the bounty of his country, a pension—'a badge' as he called it —of honorable service; the language of kindness and gratitude which the present generation was speaking to the past.

Judge Stow was a Christian and a philanthropist. He was ever kind and benevolent to the needy. He delighted in acts of humanity and love. Mr. Stow has left to his heirs, as the fruits of his toil, industry, and enterprise, a large and extensive property in this section, but he has left a far richer legacy in the bright example of a virtuous and honorable life. He died from no

8*

protracted illness. His spirit seemed weary with old age, and it took its flight for another, and we trust happier world."

ALBERT STOW.

Albert, son of Joshua and Ruth Stow, was born May 4, 1801, and at the age of twenty-eight years showed symptoms of consumption, and was advised by his physician to try a change of climate. He went with his father to Ohio in September, expecting to spend a few weeks. The change proving unfavorable, he was too feeble to attempt the return trip, by the fatiguing stage coach (the only mode then in use) so late in the fall, when his father's business was concluded. He remained with a Mr. Wetmore, an old acquaintance from Middletown. He continued to fail until February of the next year, when he died, and was buried in Ohio. He was the only son of his parents, and a young man of fine promise. There are those still living in Middlefield to whom the memory of young Albert Stow is like the garnered fragrance of flowers.

SILAS STOW.

Silas Stow, brother of Joshua, was born in Middlefield, Dec. 21, 1773. Removed to Lowville N. Y. Was member of Congress, and President of the first Constitutional Convention of that State, and his son Horatio was President of the second. Both Joshua and Silas Stow were men of a high order of talent, and great force of character. Their father was a man of strong character, and of their mother, Joshua, in some remarks which he made at her grave, commenced by saying, "Here lies the best of mothers. She taught us not so much *what* to think as *how* to think."

OBED STOW.

Obed Stow, son of Elihu Stow, was born and settled in Middlefield. He married Anna Miller, daughter of Isaac Miller, Esq. After nine years she died, leaving four children, namely :

Warren P.

Lucy W., who married E. W. Morgan, Esq., now
  living at Ann Arbor, Mich.

William, who died at 16 years of age.

Norris C., who settled in Elyria, Ohio, and died
  at the age of 28 years.

Obed Stow afterwards married Lucy Kirby of Cromwell, who survived him. They are interred in the old yard, Middlefield.

Their children were :

Anna, who married Curtiss Bacon of Middletown, Conn.

Olive, who married Noah Merwin of Durham,
  Conn.

Mary B., who married Samuel North of Berlin,
  Conn.

Sarah J., who married Peter H. Ashton of
  Middletown, Conn.

Martha, a successful teacher for thirty years.

Obed Stow was one of the members of the Congregational Church when it was reorganized in 1808, and continued one of its officers until his death. He identified himself with the old Whig party, but never took as prominent a place in politics as his brothers. He was interested in the schools of Middlefield, and gave his influence for thorough education. It was the interest felt in schools by the early settlers of Middlefield that placed theirs in the first rank.

WARREN P. STOW.

Warren P. was an active member of the Congregational Church in Middlefield, and was much interested in the cause of education, devoting much time to the improvement of the schools. He married Elizabeth Ward, and had five children:

Delia J., who died at the age of 26 years.

William, who died in Wallingford, leaving six children.

Louisa, who married S. Cone of Meriden, Conn.

Eveline, who married and died in Meriden.

Lucy D., who married — Parker, Esq., of Ann Arbor, Michigan.

BACON.

In 1747, there were Nathaniel Bacon and Joseph Bacon in Middlefield—landholders. They were from the First Society. It is probable that Nathaniel Bacon was a son of Nathaniel Bacon, one of the first settlers in Middletown. The Bacons of Middlefield were of English origin: [The record, following, obtained lately, is from a member of the Bacon family. "Nathaniel Bacon, son of William Bacon of Stretton in the county of Rutland, England, emigrated to this country and became one of the company who settled Middletown in 1650. John was his fifth child, and John was the fifth child of the first John, whose second child was also named John. He removed to the parish of Westfield and settled near the place lately occupied by Ebenezer Bacon. *His* second child was also named John, who was born in Westfield, Jan. 22, 1751, and as my record has it 'settled in the parish of Middlefield upon the old homestall,' and married first, Grace Griswold of Wallingford, and had eight children; married second wife, Olive Atkins, daughter of Joel and Mary. This John Bacon died Sept. 17, 1804, aged 53. His third child was John, who settled in Middlefield. He was born Dec. 15, 1779, and married Amy Coe, daughter of Nathan Coe."]

Their children were:

1. Curtiss, who was born April 17, 1804.
2. William.
3. John L. } twins.
4. Lucy.   }
5. George W.

Curtiss Bacon resided in the city of Middle-

town, was sheriff of the county, and U. S.
Marshal under Presidents Pierce and Buchanan.

William and John L. were in New London
for many years, and kept there a well-known
hotel bearing the name "Bacon's Hotel."

Lucy married Oliver L. Foster, and has always
lived upon the old homestall.

George W. married Phebe Birdsey, settled in
Middlefield upon "Jackson Hill." He was a
man of courteous bearing, witty sayings, a genial
companion, and a kind neighbor. Great order
and neatness prevailed throughout any establish-
ment with which he had to do. With a smile
and kindly greeting for every one, he has been
missed from these pathways "that know him no
more forever." The record says further: "The
Bacons have been content to keep the 'even tenor'
of an honest reputation, 'along the cool seques-
tered vale of life,' none perhaps distinguished
for great and shining qualities, but realizing the
truth of the old motto which was fixed to the
escutcheon of the 'Bacon' family for many a
long century, '*mediocra firma*,'—'A stable posi-
tion in the middle station of life.'"

WILLIAM COLES.

William Coles (son of William Coles who
died in Dorchester, Mass., Oct. 26, 1810) came
to Middlefield from Dorchester about the year
1793. He settled in the part now called "Falls
District," and was for twenty-six years foreman

of the paper-mill there, and for some years one of the proprietors. Paper making was at that time in the place an important branch of industry. For a long time that part of Middlefield was called the "Paper-Mill Quarter." William Coles was born Jan. 21, 1772. Married Lois Miller (daughter of William and Chloe Miller), who was born March 31, 1772.

Their children were:

Lucy, b. Mch. 9, 1797, d. Sept. 15, 1798.
Lucy 2d, b. Feb. 8, 1799, d. Dec. 15, 1799.
William, b. April 25, 1800, d. Oct. 21, 1800.
Warren, b. Oct. 1, 1801, d. Jan. 19, 1882.
William 2d, b. May 2, 1804, d. July 30, 1804.
Sarah, b. Sept. 16, 1806, d. Nov. 13, 1806.
Julia, b. Feb. 10, 1808, d. Oct. 18, 1816.
Augustus, b. July 16, 1810, d. Dec. 18, 1875.
Lucy 3d, b. Aug. 5, 1812, d. Dec. 2, 1835.
Roswell, b. Mch. 4, 1815.

William Coles died Oct. 20, 1839, aged 68 years; Lois, his wife died Dec. 5, 1855, aged 83 years and 8 months.

WARREN COLES.

Warren, son of William and Lois Coles, married Roxy Ann Magill, Jan. 10, 1827. He settled near the old home of his father, and was engaged for some time in the manufacture of paper. In middle life he went to California, at the time of the gold excitement, where he remained fourteen years. The last years of his life were spent at the home of his son, Valerius Coles, in the "Falls District" near to the home of his childhood. He died Jan. 19, 1882, aged 81 years.

The children of Warren and Roxy Ann Coles were:

Valeria, who married Levi Parsons Hubbard.

Valerius, m. Angeline Norton.

Erskine, m. Lydia Thorne.

Lois Euphrasia, m. George Kendall; d. April 21, 1864.

Adelaide M., m. L. V. Connover.

AUGUSTUS COLES.

Augustus, son of William and Lois Coles, removed to the city of Middletown. He married Nancy Hubbard, daughter of Enoch Hubbard, April 14, 1837.

Children:

George A., who married Augusta, daughter of William H. Atkins, Oct. 11, 1860.

Roswell W., m. Julia A. Morse of Springfield, Mass., Oct. 10, 1866.

Josephine A., m. Horace Southmayd of Middletown, Oct. 14, 1863; d. April 24, 1874.

Alice H., m. Eugene S. Belden, Apr. 18, 1866.

ROSWELL COLES.

Roswell, youngest of ten children of William and Lois Miller Coles, was born March 4, 1815, and left home at the age of 16 to learn the trade of a blacksmith. This was in 1831. In 1843 he went to New York State, where he settled in Napanock, town of Wawarsing, Ulster Co. He married Apher Carney, July 3, 1845.

To them were born two sons and one daughter, namely:

William, who married Anna Cantine.

Warren, who m. Mary E. Pettibone.

Lucetta, now living in Whitman Co., Washington Territory.

After the death of Apher Carney, his first wife, he married Elizabeth Vanderlyn, of Fallsburg, Sullivan Co., New York.

LUCY COLES.

Lucy, daughter of William and Lois Coles, was born Aug. 5, 1812, and died Dec. 2, 1835. She was the third Lucy in the family, and was a young woman of admirable character and greatly beloved. She died at the age of 23, regretted by all who knew her.

CAPT. WILLIAM WARD.

Capt. William Ward was a landholder in 1747. He was probably from the First Society, as Wards were among the first settlers in Middletown. His house stood on the west street. He died in 1786. There were several other Ward families; they might have sprung from the said William. There were Dr. Asher Ward, William Ward, Jr., Timothy Ward, Capt. James T. Ward, James Ward 2d, and Sylvester Ward. All of these families but one, are gone.

9

WILLIAM WARD.

William Ward, son of William Ward, married Rhoda Bacon of Westfield. Their children were·
William, who lived in Middlefield.
Caroline, who married Nathaniel Hook, and moved West.
Maria, who married Alfred Bailey.

CAPT. JAMES WARD.

Capt. James Ward married Elizabeth, daughter of Ichabod Miller. He lived in the North District near the "Old Burying-ground." Afterward he moved to a house near where the Methodist Parsonage now stands.
The children of James and Elizabeth Ward were :
James 2d, who married Eunice Birdsey.
Phineas, unmarried.
Reuben.
Irena, died young.
Elizabeth, who m. William Birdsey.
Martha, who m. a Brainard, and moved to the "Black River Country."

JAMES WARD 2D.

James Ward 2d, married Eunice Birdsey, and lived near the center of Middlefield. Eunice Birdsey Ward died Jan. 30, 1858. The following is clipped from a Middletown paper. "In this town, Middlefield Society, Mrs. Eunice Ward, widow of the late James Ward, aged nearly 88 years. She was a worthy member of the Congregational Church in this place, and was much loved and respected by a large circle of relatives and acquaintances. She was cheerful and social in temperament, and passionately fond of flowers."

The children of James and Eunice Ward were:

Almira, still living at the old home (1883).

Eunice, who married Richard M. Bailey.

Lucina.

Amelia, who m. 1st, Timothy Coe; 2d, John Smith.

James, who m.

Electa, who m. William T. Boardman of Westfield.

Irena, who m. Peter Ashton.

Elizabeth, died young.

John, died in infancy.

CAPT. OLIVER BAILEY.

Oliver Bailey, son of Oliver Bailey of Haddam, Conn., was born in 1763, and settled in Middlefield not far from a century ago. He was one of fifteen children, three of whom settled in Massachusetts, one in Connecticut (Middlefield), and eleven in Pennsylvania.

The children of Oliver were six sons and one daughter, namely:

Alfred,	Roswell,
Ira,	Minerva,
Richard M.,	Russell.
Oliver,	

CAPT. ALFRED BAILEY.

Alfred Bailey, son of Oliver Bailey, was born Sept. 20, 1791, and died May 14, 1871. He married Maria, daughter of William Ward. She was born March 18, 1795, and died May 20, 1881. Their children were:

Almira W.,	William Ward,
Lavinia M.,	Mary Lucina,
Louisa C.,	Rhoda A.,
Alfred M.,	Phebe C.

RICHARD M. BAILEY.

Richard, son of Oliver, married Eunice Ward and lived in the Falls district, Middlefield, where for a considerable term of years he owned and operated the saw-mill at the "Falls."

The children of Richard M. and Eunice Ward were:

Mariette, who died at the age of eleven.

Eveline, who married Ozias Merriman.

Ward, who m. Marion Inglis.

Eugene, who m. Esther Rockwell.

Richard M. Bailey died January, 1879.

COMFORT HALL.

Comfort Hall, although not born in Middlefield, and living just outside its limits, yet was identified with its history of more than half a century ago. He was one of the early Methodists, and one of the original trustees of the M. E. Church in Middlefield. He was of the old type of Methodism, earnest, zealous, a devoted attendant at church, and his home always open to entertain Methodist preachers. There are many living in Middlefield who have a vivid recollection of "Uncle Comfort's" fervent prayers. He was born in Wallingford, Feb. 25, 1773, and died Nov. 20, 1855, aged 82. He married Jemima Bacon of Westfield, who was born February, 1775, and died Feb. 24, 1847, aged 72 years.

The children of Comfort and Jemima Hall were :

Sylvester,	Amos,
Harley,	Cornelius,
Miles,	Seth,
Abia,	Johnson Comfort,
Aaron,	Winsell Bacon.

JOHN DICKENSON.

John Dickenson was not one of the early settlers of Middlefield, yet his connection reaches back nearly a century. He lived to be over 90 years of age, and in his boyhood learned his trade (that of shoemaker) of Obed Stow. For some time after his first marriage he lived near the "Falls" in that district. It was here that his wife died in the "sickly year," of typhus fever. Subsequently he bought and occupied the house and farm near that of Thomas Atkins. The place originally belonged to the "Wetmores," some of the early settlers. In middle life John Dickenson spent some time as a merchant, ped-

9*

dling in the South. Late in life he sold his farm and spent his remaining years with his daughter, Mrs. Charles Gabrielle, in Colchester.

His children by his first wife were:

Samuel, who died unmarried.

Mary, who married Charles Gabrielle.

For his second wife John Dickenson married Celia Galpin, the mother of Emily Galpin (who married Capt. Henry Bacon of Middletown), and of William Galpin of Middletown (who in earlier life was for a long time in business in Lexington, Kentucky).

The children of John and Celia Dickenson were:

Adeline, who married Rev. William R. Johnson.

John, who m.

RECORD OF THE DEAD OF MIDDLEFIELD,

FROM 22D OF MAY, 1761.

IN ALPHABETICAL ORDER.

KEPT BY HEZEKIAH HALE, JOSHUA STOW, AND OTHERS.

———

Allen, Obadiah's wife, died Oct. 25, 1764.
Allen, Sarah,   "   May 17, 1770.
Allen, Margaret, wid.,   "   Sept. 16, 1771.
Allen, Ebenezer's child, "   Feb. 13, 1772.
Allen, Obadiah,   "   July 13, 1783.
Augur, Justus' child (still born), March 14, 1784.
Atkins, Abigail, died April 16, 1784.
Allen, Ebenezer's child, died Feb. 7, 1785.
Allen, Ebenezer's child,   "   Sept. 19, 1786.
Augur, Prosper's child,   "   Dec. 17, 1794.
Allen, Ebenezer's wife,   "   April 7, 1807.
Augur, Thankful, wife of Prosper Augur, age 69 years,
          died Sept. 16, 1825.
Augur, Phineas, age 37 years, died Nov. 18, 1825.
Ashton, Peter's (twin child), died, 1825.
Aston, Deroy, child of Joseph, "   1833.
Augur, Prosper, age 81 years, "Dec. 16, 1836.
Aston, Joseph, died May 6, 1842.
Atkins, Emily Ruth, child of Thomas, age 4 years and
          4 months; died July 22, 1844.
Augur, Polly.
Abel, William, died at Colchester.
Atkins, Lucy, wife of Thomas, (suddenly) died Oct. 13,
          1859.

Bradly, Leaming's child, died Sept. 15, 1764.

Bacon, Anna, died Nov. 12, 1765.

Birdsey, Gershom's child, died Dec. 6, 1766.

Bacon, Nathaniel's wife, " April 11, 1769.

Birdsey, Gershom's child, " Dec. 18, 1768.

Bacon, Nathaniel, " Nov. 8, 1769.

Brocket, Sarah, widow, " Nov. 5, 1769.

Barnes, Ezekiel's child, " Jan. 2, 1772.

Birdsey, Benjamin's child, " Feb. 17, 1773.

Birdsey, David's child (still born), March 15, 1773.

Benedict, Rev. Abner's child, died July 7, 1774.

Birdsey, David's child, died April 28, 1775.

Bartlett, Ephraim's child, " July 11, 1775.

Birdsey, Benjamin's wife, " Aug. 12, 1775.

Bow, Peleg, died Aug. 18, 1776.

Bartlett, Ephraim (in New York), — 21, 1776.

Black, Mrs., died April 10, 1780.

Boardman, Samuel Allyn, died Sept. 22. 1780.

Birdsey, Gershom's child, " May 16, 1781.

Bartlett, James' child, " May 16, 1783.

Butler, Timothy's child, " June 9, 1783.

Babcock, Samuel, " Nov. 2, 1783.

Birdsey, Seth (killed by fall of a tree), Feb. 16, 1784.

Babcock, Dorcas, wid., died Feb. 21, 1784.

Brown, John (crazy), " Dec. 6, 1787.

Birdsey, Benjamin, " Aug. 28, 1789.

Birdsey, Gershom, " Nov. 17, 1789.

Birdsey, John's wife, " March 20, 1791.

Bagby, David of Chatham (found dead), May 13, 1791.

Birdsey, Abel's wife, died Dec. 19, 1791.

Birdsey, John (an early settler in Middlefield), died
    June 17, 1798.

Birdsey, John Jr.'s child, died Oct. 6, 1801.

Bradley, Widow, " Dec. 20, 1802.

Birdsey, Elihu II.'s child, " Oct. 21, 1803.

Birdsey, Capt. David's wife, died July 23, 1804.

Birdsey, John Jr.'s child,   "   Dec. 22, 1804.

Birdsey, John the 2d, age 76 years, died Mar. 9, 1807.

Birdsey, John Jr.'s child, died May 11, 1807.

Bailey, Isaac's child,   "   March 2, 1808.

Birdsey, John Jr.'s wife,   "   Aug. 25, 1808.

Birdsey, Elizabeth, wife of William, died July 27, 1814.

Birdsey, William's child, died Dec., 1814.

Butler, Widow, of the city of Middletown, died Feb. 9, 1815.

Bailey, Oliver, Capt., age 54, died May 27, 1817.

Birdsey, Alva, son of Seth B., age 18, died Aug. 1, 1817.

Birdsey, Capt. David's wife Abigail,   "   May 27, 1818.

Birdsey, Widow Abigail, age 74,   "   April 5, 1822.

Birdsey, William, died June 4, 1823.

Birdsey, Rachel, wife of Abel the 2d, died June 18, 1823.

Birdsey, Capt. Seth, age 48, died Aug. 30, 1825.

Birdsey, Capt. David, age 77, died Sept. 12, 1825.

Birdsey, Benjamin, age 39,   "   Oct. 20, 1825.

Birdsey, Abel, son of William, "   1828.

Birdsey, Abel, age about 82,   "   1832.

Birdsey, Almon's wife, died Nov. 20, 1832.

Birdsey, Almon's child, "   Jan. 20, 1833.

Bradley, Catherine,   "   April 18, 1833.

Bacon, William's child, "   April 29, 1833.

Birdsey, John Jr., age about 16, died May 8, 1833.

Birdsey, Ruth, wid., age 87,   "   May 12, 1834.

Birdsey, Amner, wid., age 87,   "   March 5, 1835.

Bailey, Maryette, age 11, daughter of Richard, died Aug. 4, 1835.

Bacon, George's child, died Sept. 15, 1835.

Brainard, Minerva, age 27, died April 6, 1836.

Bailey, Amner, wid., age,   "   Jan. 13, 1838.

Birdsey, Hiram's child,   "   Jan., 1838.

Bailey, Eunice, wife of Richard M., died Nov. 29, 18 .

Birdsey, Henry, son of Samuel B., died July 16, 1842.
Birdsey, Nancy. wid. of Abel B., " 1846.
Birdsey, Samuel, age 75, died Aug. 7, 1850.
Birdsey, John, age 69, " Nov. 13, 1856.
Birdsey, Emerson, age, " March 20, 1864.
Bailey, Sylvester C., age, " Jan. 26, 1864.
Birdsey, Ruth, age 89, " unmarried, 1866.
Bennett, Jane M., wife of P. W. B., age 36, died
    Jan. 25, 1863.
Birdsey, Phineas.
Chilson, Asaph's wife, died Sept. 5, 1761.
Coe, Reuben's wife, " Nov. 17, 1766.
Camp, Edward's child, " April 14, 1768.
Coe, Ezra, son of David, " Dec. 2, 1771.
Coe, Abigail, wid., " July 16, 1775.
Coe, Nathan's child, " Sept. 10, 1776.
Coe, Dea. Joseph's wife, " Sept. 22, 1776.
Clark, Samuel, " Jan. 27, 1777.
Clark, Samuel's child, " Feb. 10, 1777.
Coe, John's child. " Dec. 1, 1778.
Coe, Seth's child, " Feb. 13, 1779.
Cone, Beriah's child, died June 5, 1779.
Clark, Widow, " July 15, 1779.
Coe, Elizabeth, " April 27, 1782.
Camp, Bela's wife, " Nov. 9, 1782.
Coe, Deacon Joseph, " June 10, 1784.
Coe, David, Jr.'s child, " Jan. 7, 1787.
Coe, Eli's child (still born), died Feb. 12, 1787.
Coe, Reuben's wife, " April 17, 1788.
Coe, Nathan, Jr.'s child, " Feb. 19, 1789.
Coe, Sanford, " May 9, 1789.
Coe, Nathan, Jr.'s wife, " Feb. 12, 1794.
Clark, Daniel, " April 8, 1794.
Cone, Elisha, Jr., " July 16, 1794.
Camp, Edward, Ensign, " Feb. 6, 1795.

Coe, Elisha, son Edwin,   died Nov. 22, 1796.
Coe, Nathan,   "   Dec. 10, 1796.
Coe, Eli's child,   "   Jan. 23, 1798.
Camp, Lemuel,   "   July 21, 1798.
Coles, William's child,   "   Sept. 15, 1798.
Coe, Joseph's child,   "   Oct. 21, 1798.
     Do.   "   Oct. 26, 1798.
Coles, William's child,   "   Dec. 15, 1799.
Coe, Seth, Jr. (Black River), "   June 17, 1800.
Coles, William's child,   "   Oct. 21, 1800.
Cone, Hannah,   "   April 30, 1800.
Coles, Widow,   "   Sept. 9, 1801.
Coe, Mary,   "   June 12, 1803.
Chilson, Hope,   "   Nov. 3, 1803.
Coe, Camp's wife (Mary Crowell), died March 3, 1804.
Coles, William's child,   "   July 30, 1804.
Coe, Camp's child,   "   Oct. 7, 1805.
Curtis, Benjamin's child (of Marlboro), died — 22, 1805.
Curtis, James, blown up in powder-mill, Feb. 18, 1806.
Coles, William's child, died Nov. 12, 1806.
Coe, Capt. David,   "   Jan. 15, 1807.
Cotton, Lucy,   "   March 1, 1808.
Coe, Hannah, wife of Capt. David Coe, died Oct. 16, 1808.
Coe, Eli, Jr.'s child, died July 17, 1812.
Cone, Elisha,   "   Sept. 30, 1812.
Camp, Fairchild's child, died Dec. 30, 1812.
Coe, Sophia, daughter of Col. Elisha Coe, died Nov. 8, 1814.
Coe, Roswell, son of Col. Elisha Coe, age 18, died Dec. 18, 1814.
Caples, Jesse's child (colored), died Dec. 1814.
Curtis, Edward,   "   Sept. 30, 1816.
Coles, William's daughter, Julia, " Oct. 18, 1816.
Camp, Esther, widow, aged 93, " Dec. 27, 1817.

Coe, Eli's child, Seth, age 6,　died May 16, 1818.

Cora, Hannah, Widow, age 75, "　Dec. 10, 1820.

Chapin, Josiah's infant child,　"　1821.

Coe, Linus' child, Harriet Sophia, age 10 months, died March, 1821.

Caples, Jesse's wife (colored), drowned at Middle Haddam, Nov. 17, 1821.

Chapin, Jonah's child (still born), Nov. 20, 1821.

Coe, Linus' infant child,　died Dec. 18, 1821.

Coe, Cyrus, age 24,　"　Sept. 22, 1822.

Coe, Dana's child,　"　1822.

Cone, Widow, over 78 years,　"　Feb. 18, 1823.

Carter, Asaph (colored),　"　June 12, 1823.

Caples, Emily, daughter of Jesse (colored), died March 12, 1824.

Clark, Hezekiah, age 18, blown up in powder-mill, March, 1825.

Cook, Hezekiah's child, age 1, died Jan. 22, 1826.

Coe, Rachel, wife of Elihu, age 43, died March 13, 1826.

Clark, William, Jr.'s child, age 4, "　May 13, 1826.

Clark, William, age 29,　"　Nov. 6, 1826.

Coe, Cornwell, age 40,　"　Oct. 5, 1825.

Cook, Hezekiah, age 37,　"　Nov. 15, 1826.

Cook, Benjamin, age 24,　"　April 10, 1827.

Coe, Hannah, wife of Capt. Bela Coe, age 47, died Aug. 9, 1827.

Coe, Linus' child (scalded), died May, 1828.

Caples, Jesse's child (colored), died 1828.

Coe, Joseph, age 76, died July 9, 1828.

Coe, Henry, son of Linus, age 7, died Aug. 1, 1829.

Coe, Seth, age 73, died Sept. 26, 1829.

Clark, Widow Amos' child, died 1830.

Coe, Elizabeth, wid. of Joseph Coe, died 1830.

Coe, Elisha, Col., age 68,　"　Dec. 1, 1831.

Coe, Mary, wid. of Seth,　"　Jan. 1, 1832.

Coe, Betsey, wife of Linus, age 37, died Oct. 17, 1833.

Coe, Laura Stow, wife of Curtis Coe, age 43, died Feb. 16, 1834.

Coe, Eli, Esq., age 77, died Friday, March 27, 1835.

Coe, Hannah, age 21,   "   May 13, 1835.

Coe, Elizabeth, wid. of Col. Elisha Coe, died June, 1835.

Coe, Charlotte, daughter of Cornwell Coe, died Sept. 21, 1835.

Coles, Lucy, daughter of William, age 23, died Dec. 2, 1835.

Camp, Wid. E., died 1835.

Coe, Dency, daughter of Cornwell Coe, age 19, died (of consumption) Sept. 2, 1836.

Coe, Camp's wife, died Sept. 7, 1837.

Coles, William, age 68, died Oct. 20, 1839.

Coe, Dennis, age 39,   "   Aug. 9, 18 .

Coe, Bela, Capt., age 63, "   Oct. 4, 1841.

Coe, Timothy,   "   Sept. 16, 1842.

Coe, Edwin, son of William, died July, 1843.

Coe, Rachel, wife of Eli, age 83, died May 27, 1844.

Cook, Lucius, died April 12, 1845.

Coe, Delia, daughter of Col. E. Coe, died Sept., 1846.

Coe, Camp, died April, 1846.

Coe, Eli, age 62, died Jan. 30, 1847.

Coe, Polly, wid. of Cornwell (died in city), Sept. 20, 1849.

Coe, Selena, daughter of Enoch Coe, age 16.

Coe, William W.

Coe, ——, son of Ebenezer Coe.

Coles, Lois, wid. of Wm., age 83, died Dec. 5, 1855.

Coe, Henry, son of Luther (died in Staddle Hill), 1855.

Coe, Cyrenus, son of Luther (died in Meriden), 1858.

Coe, Wilbur, son of John C. (twin), age 5 months.

Coe, Elihu, died Aug. 24, 1859.

Coe, Eunice, wife of Joseph, age 77, died Oct. 1, 1861.

Coe, Joseph, Capt., age 91, died at his son's in Westfield, Oct. 1, 1874.

Coe, Curtis, age 89, died July 6, 1875.

Coe, Levi, Col., age 75, died Jan. 15, 1864.

Coe, Hannah, age 21, died (of consumption) May 13, 1835.

Coe, Charlotte, age 15, died (of consumption) Sept. 23, 1835.

Coe, Mary, age 19, died (of consumption) Sept. 21, 1836.

Dowd, Isaac, died May 27, 1769.

Denison, Rev. Joseph, age 31, died Feb. 12, 1770.

Dickinson, John, died Aug. 3, 1785.

Dickinson, John's child, died Aug. 7, 1807.

Doxy, Old Mrs., died July 25, 1811.

Dickinson, Polly, wife of John Dickinson, died July, 1825.

Derby, Sarah, wife of Patrick, age 30, died Oct. 17, 1825.

Derby, Eliza, wife of Samuel,   " Aug. 26, 1841.

Dickinson, Celia, wife of John, age 73, " Dec. 23, 1865.

Dickinson, John, age 92, died Sept. 23, 1878.

Eggleston, James' child,   " Dec. 25, 1771.

Eggleston, James' wife,   " March 9, 1872.

Evarts, Widow, age 70,   " ' Sept. 8, 1825.

Eaton, Hezekiah, died (of consumption) 1861.

Eaton, Lydia E., daughter of Hezekiah, age 7, died Oct. 14, 18 .

Ferry, Katie E., daughter of John, age 4, died Mar. 9, 1859.

Ferry, John's child, died Sept. 4, 1857.

Ferry, John (drowned in Staddle Hill), 1860.

Flushing, Owen's child, died Jan. 11, 1766.

Flushing, Owen's child,   " Jan. 1, 1773.

Freeman, David's child,   " Aug. 12, 1776.

Fluskey, Daniel, died (at Torrington) Oct. 11, 1789.

Freeman, Hannah, wife of David, died Aug. 11, 1802.

Fluskey, Harriet, daughter of James, died Jan. 4, 1815.

Ford, Mabel, died (of measles in her teens) Jan. 17, 1816.

Freeman, Blanford (colored slave), age 75, died Dec., 1818.

Freeman, Philemon (col.), age 70, died May 18, 1820.

Freeman, Peter (col.), born in Africa, age 80 or 90, died Dec., 1820.

Ferren, Sally, age 56, died Oct. 9, 1826.

Freeman, David, age 81, " Dec. 5, 1826.

Green, Susan, daughter of Samuel Green, died May 26, 1763.

Griffen, Samuel's wife, died Nov. 18, 1764.

Green, Samuel's child, " May 3, 1765.

Green, Samuel's wife, " April 4, 1767.

Green, Samuel's 2d wife, " April 4, 1769.

Griffen, Samuel's child, " Aug. 6, 1771.

Green, Samuel's 3d wife, " Feb. 2, 1773.

Green, Samuel, " July 10, 1775.

Guild, Jeremiah's child, " Jan. 19, 1776.

Guild, Samuel's child, " Feb. 23, 1776.

Gibbs, Amasa's child, " Jan. 10, 1778.

Gay, Lasher, died (of small-pox) April 18, 1778.

Gould, Elizabeth, died Nov. 20, 1778.

Guild, Samuel's child, died March 23, 1784.

Griffen, Samuel's child, " May 26, 1787.

Griffen, Samuel's 3d wife, died April 18, 1788.

Guild, Eleanor, wid., " March 21, 1792.

Goodrich, Samuel's wife, " Jan. 20, 1809.

Gouge, Old Mr., " Jan. 16, 1813.

Gay, John, from Vermont, died Aug. 26, 1824.

Geer, George, age 46, " Sept. 26, 1833.

Geer, Samuel, age 56, " Feb. 7, 1835.

Grover, Jared's child, " May 6, 1845.

Geer, Elizabeth, wife of George, died Nov. 14, 1845.

Geer, Charles' child, died 1846.

Geer, Submit, age 68, died Dec. 25, 1852.
Hubbard, Ebenezer's wife, died May 22, 1761.
Hawley, Samuel Stow's child, died May 13, 1762.
Hawley, Hope, died Jan. 24, 1763.
Hubbard, Elijah's child, died Sept. 9, 1767.
Hale, Abigail, wid.,   " March 5, 1770.
Hale, Hezekiah's daughter, Eunice, died Jan. 13, 1770.
Hale, Joseph, son to Hezekiah,   " Nov. 20, 1770.
Harris, Sarah, wid., died Jan. 1, 1775.
Howard, Mary, wid., " Sept. 5, 1775.
Higby, Edward,   " Nov. 21, 1775.
Hawley, Samuel Stow's child, died Jan. 24, 1776.
Hubbard, Ebenezer,   " March, 1776.
Hale, Hezekiah's wife,   " March, 1776.
Hubbard, Elijah's child (still born), Aug. 16, 1776.
Hubbard, Elijah's wife, died Dec. 7, 1776.
Hubbard, Lydia, wid.,   " March 28, 1779.
Hale, Joseph's wife,   " Jan. 22, 1779.
Hubbard, Jedediah,   " Dec. 10, 1780.
Hale, Hezekiah's 2d wife, died Aug. 29, 1782.
Hale, Joseph, 2d,   " July 3, 1785.
Hand, Ebenezer,   " March 14, 1787.
Hale, Joseph,   " May 24, 1790.
Hawley, Seth's child,   " Jan. 12, 1792.
Hand, Benjamin's child,   " April 18, 1793.
Hand, Benjamin's child,   " June 8, 1793.
Hall, Jabez, Capt.,   " July 12, 1797.
Hawley, Samuel Stow,   " Dec. 20, 1798.
Hawley, Ruth, wid.,   " Aug. 9, 1801.
Hand, Benjamin's child,   " Aug. 30, 1801.
Hawley, Miller's child,   " Aug. 16, 1802.
Hickling, Katy, wife of John, died Aug. 8, 1802.
Hambleton, Widow,   " Nov. 8, 1802.
Hand, Benjamin's child,   " June 5, 1805.
Hoadley, Abel (deranged, drowned) June 12, 1805.

Hall, Widow, died Oct. 15, 1805.

Hawley, Nancy's child, died May 13, 1807.

Hough, Aaron's child,   "   June 30, 1807.

Henry, Widow,   "   Nov. 8, 1807.

Hamlin, George, died (fit) July 27, 1808.

Hoadley, Dr. Jehiel's wife, age 57, died Jan. 1, 1810.

Hoadley, Dr. Jehiel, age 66,   "   March 2, 1810.

Hawley, Christopher, died Sept. 9, 1812.

Hale, Hezekiah,   "   Nov. 18, 1813.

Hotchkiss, infant child, "   Feb. 1, 1816.

Hawley, Abigail, wife of Samuel H., age 59, died June, 1817.

Hawley, Samuel, age 60, died May 14, 1820.

Hall, Elijah, died Jan. 16, 1822.

Hubbard, Submit, age 83, died March 2, 1825.

Hale, Hezekiah, age 48,   "   Oct. 31, 1825.

Hubbard, Henry,   "   Dec. 27, 1834.

Hall, Miles' wife,   "   Sept., 1839.

Hale, Julia, wife of Joseph, died July 11, 1845.

Hale, Phineas, age 26, died (of consumption) Jan. 20, 1845.

Hale, Roswell, died (of consumption).

Hersey, Mila, daughter of Seth Miller.

Hale, Nancy, wid. of Hezekiah, age 93 yrs. and 4 mos., died Aug. 31, 1878.

Hale, Joseph, age 75, died at Cuyahoga, Ohio (buried in Middlefield), Aug. 16, 1855.

Ives, Noel, age 73, died March 27, 1838.

Ives, Eunice, wid. of Noel, age 80, died 1855.

Ives, Sherman, age 67, died Oct. 21, 1871.

Kimball, A. Tyler's son, "   June 17, 1792.

Kimball, Wid. Their,   "   March 25, 1807.

Kenyon, John,   "   March 22, 1810.

Kimball, Ira, age 26,   "   Aug. 13, 1817.

Kimball, Asa's child, age 3 months, died Oct. 28, 1821.

10*

Kimball, Asa's infant child, died March 8, 1828.

Kenyon's twin children (on Col. Coe's farm), died Nov., 1833.

Kimball, A. Tyler, age 77, died May 5, 1834.

Kimball, Wid. Sarah, age 78, " Nov. 9, 1839.

Kelsey, Cyrus' child, age about 3, died April 11, 1844.

Kimball, Asa, age 80, died Dec. 25, 1874.

Kimball, Mary, wife of Asa, died Feb. 4, 1877.

Leaming, Matthias' child, " Nov. 23, 1762.

Lyman, John, died May 21, 1763.

Long, Widow, " June 14, 1764.

Lewis, Rebecca's child, died Feb. 13, 1767.

Latimer, Elizabeth's child, died Jan. 3, 1773.

Learning, Aaron's child, " Dec. 28, 1775.

Lyman, Phineas, " Sept. 13, 1776.

Lyman, Dr. Elihu's child, " April 27, 1780.

Lyman, Dr. Elihu's child, " Nov. 24, 1781.

Lucas, David's child, " April 23, 1795.

Lung, Jerusha, " Jan. 11, 1796.

Lyman, Phineas, " April 5, 1799.

Lee, Elijah's child, " Sept. 28, 1800.

Lee, Elijah's child, " Oct. 21, 1801.

Loomis, Asahel's child (still born), 1802.

Lucas, David's child (still born), July 19, 1807.

Loomis, Old Mr., died Sept. 16, 1807.

Lee, Elijah's wife, " Dec. 30, 1810.

Lyman, David, Jr. (died in Vermont), Mar. 15, 1811.

Lee, Elijah, died May 3, 1811.

Lyman, Alanson's wife, died Jan. 13, 1814.

Lyman, David, Col., age 69, died Feb. 28, 1815.

Lyman, Alfred's child, age 5 mos., died Mar. 15, 1821.

Lyman, Alfred, infant child, " April 10, 1824.

Lyman, Cornelia, died May 13, 1824.

Lyman, wid. of Elihu, age 26, died Aug. 14, 1825.

Lucas, Orrin, age 25, " Jan. 22, 1826.

Lyman, Phineas, son of William, age 18, died Feb. 13, 1826.

Lyman, Adaline, daughter of Wm., died Aug. 26, 1826.

Lyman, Andrew, age 36, died May 10, 1819.

Lyman, Alma, " Oct., 1830.

Lyman, Sally, wid., age 78, died Feb. 29, 1831.

Lyman, Eliza, age about 16, " April 25, 1832.

Lyman, Esther, wid., age 77, " May 4, 1836.

Lyman, Alfred, " May 4, 1843.

Lyman, Aunt Anna, age 85, " Aug. 25, 1844.

Lucas, William's wife and child, died 1846.

Lucas, Josiah, died June 9, 1851.

Lyman, Elihu, age 23, died Aug. 26, 1848.

Lyman, Adeline, age 20, " July 5, 1859.

Lucas, Mary, wid. of Josiah, age 76, died July 5, 1870.

Lee, Roswell, age 66, died Jan. 31, 1873.

Markes, William's child, died April 27, 1763.

Miller, Giles' wife, " June 4, 1764.

Miller, William's child, " Feb. 5, 1765.

Miller, Benjamin, first settler in Middlefield, age 76, died July 9, 1769.

McCough, Timothy's child, died March 22, 1771.

Miller, E. Joseph's wife, " June 2, 1771.

Mark, Samuel, died Dec. 8, 1772.

Miller, Capt. David's wife, died Oct. 9, 1773.

Miller, Jacob's child, " July 6, 1774.

Miller, Capt. David's wife's child, died Dec. 1, 1775.

Miller, Richard's child, " Aug. 9, 1776.

Mark, Abigail, died Nov. 25, 1776.

Miller, Joseph, son of Amos, died Dec. 23, 1776.

Miller, Amos, died Jan. 17, 1777.

Miller, Jacob's child, died March 25, 1777.

Miller, David, son of Amos, died Nov. 27, 1777.

Miller, Richard's child, " Dec. 22, 1777.

Miller, William Jr.'s child, died Aug. 28, 1778.

Miller, William's wife, died Oct. 23, 1778.
Mark, William's wife, " Nov. 8, 1778.
Miller, Jacob's child, (born and died) May 25, 1779.
Meigs, Ezekiel, died Dec. 19, 1779.
Miller, Richard, " June 28, 1780.
Miller, Capt. Timothy, died March 1, 1783.
Miller, Jacob's child, (still born) May 21, 1785.
Miller, Benjamin, (drowned at Newfields) April 17, 1786.
Miller, Dea. Ichabod's wife, died Aug. 22, 1787.
Miller, Ambrose's child, " Feb. 17, 1788.
Miller, Dea. Ichabod, " Aug. 9, 1788.
Miller, Hezekiah's child, " Oct. 18, 1788.
Miller, Elisha's child, " -- 27, 1788.
Marks, Ruth, " Dec. 23, 1788.
Miller, Capt. David, " Feb. 28, 1789.
Miller, William's wife, " Jan. 5, 1790.
Miller, Elisha's child, " July 6, 1790.
Miller, Hezekiah's child, " Feb. 24, 1792.
Miller, Dea. Giles' wife, " Feb. 3, 1793.
Miller, Abigail, Wid., " Sept. 13, 1793.
Miller, D. Brainerd's child, " Sept. 23, 1793.
Miller, Ichabod, Jr., " Sept. 20, 1794. --
Miller, Lucy, died Nov. 3, 1794.
Miller, Isaac's daughter, Cornelia, died Mar. 18, 1795.
Miller, Curtis, son of Isaac, died March 31, 1795.
Miller, William, Jr. (killed in saw-mill), Nov. 2, 1795.
Miller, Hannah, wid., died Sept. 3, 1796.
Miller, Hezekiah's child (still born), May 26, 1800.
Miller, Richard (died at Savannah, Georgia), April 4, 1802.
Miller, Dea. Giles, age 77, died March 4, 1804.
Miller, William, died March 1, 1804.
Miller, Ambrose, " Jan. 9, 1805.
Miller, Joel, " Nov. 11, 1805.

Mark, Susanna, died June 3, 1807.

Miller, Widow,   " Sept. 12, 1807.

Miller, David's child, died in Granville, Mar. 22, 1808.

Mark, William,   " May 1, 1809.

Miller, Hezekiah's child, died May 5, 1809.

Miller, Asher, son to Giles, died Oct. 14, 1809.

Melony, Nancy's child,   " May 15, 1810.

Miller, Chauncey, son of Ambrose, died Oct. 5, 1813.

Miller, Jacob, Jr., age 35, died (of measles) Feb. 5, 1816.

Miller, Jennie, wife of Giles, age 52, died Nov. 17, 1816.

Miller, Isaac, Esq., age 79,   "   July 27, 1817.

Miller, Seth Jun.'s child (age 3 mos.), died Mar. 8, 1819.

Miller, Joel Bradley, age 31, (killed by fall of tree) Jan. 3, 1820.

Miller, Joshua's child, died Nov. 22, 1821.

Miller, Ichabod, age 84 yrs. and 10 mos., died March 12, 1824.

Miller, John W.'s wife, age 41, died July, 1825.

Miller, Horace, age 37,   "   Aug. 7, 1825.

Miller, wid. of Wm., age 83,   "   Oct. 18, 1825.

Miller, Joseph, son of Seth, age 35, died Nov. 11, 1825.

Miller, Sarah, wife of Hezekiah, age 60, died Nov. 28, 1825.

Miller, Sarah, daughter of Horace, age 8 years, died Dec. 19, 1825.

Miller, Ruth, wid. of Jacob, age 47, died Jan. 9, 1826.

Miller, Jeremiah's daughter, age 12, " Nov. 4, 1826.

Miller, Elizabeth, daughter of Ichabod, age 62, Oct. 21, 1827.

Miller, Miranda, wife of Col. Amos M., died May, 1828.

Miller, Ichabod, Capt., died Nov., 1829. —

Miller, Seth, Capt.,   "   1830.

Miller, Seth,   " April, 1831.

Miller, Elizabeth, wid., age 83, died Dec. 3, 1831. _

Miller, Joshua, died July 4, 1832.

Miller, Elihu's infant child, died March, 1833.

Miller, Amanda, daughter of Elisha, Jr., died Oct. 14, 1833.

Miller, Hannah, wid., age 91, died Dec. 17, 1833.

Miller, William's (infant child), died 1833.

Miller, Hannah, wife of Capt. Seth, died Aug., 1834.

Miller, Nancy, child of David B., " Oct. 1, 1835.

Miller, Almon's infant child, " Dec. 7, 1835.

Miller, Jacob, age 92, died April 8, 1836.

Miller, Elisha, age 89 (nearly), died Feb. 14, 1839.

Miller, Giles, age 58, died Nov. 26, 1839.

Miller, Henry W., age 10, son of Almon, died Aug. 8, 1841.

Miller, Adah, died Oct. 3, 1842.

Miller, Amos' child, died Feb. 27, 1843.

Miller, Cornelia, wife of David B., died Sept., 1844.

Miller, Esther, age 87, died Oct. 20, 1845.

Miller, Charity, wid. of Seth M., died Nov. 15, 1845.

Miller, Parsons, son of Elisha, age 25, died Mar. 1, 1847.

Mix, Sally, age 63, died March 13, 1847.

Miller, Elihu, age 59, (died suddenly) Aug. 21, 1847.

Miller, Jeremiah.

Miller, Sarah, wid. of Capt. Ichabod.

Miller, Louisa (died at Miles Hall's), 1854.

Miller, Seth's child (at the Abel house), 1854.

Miller, Joshua, died 1853.

Miller, Nelson's child (Selena), died Aug. 6, 1853.

Merchant, Eli, died April 5, 1858.

Miller, Emily M., daughter of Benjamin M., died April 1, 1859.

Miller, Roxanna, wife of Jesse M., age 33, died Aug. 19, 1860.

Miller, Mary, age 77, died 1861.

Miller, Clara, wid. of Giles, died July 14, 1862.

Miller, Asher, age 59, died July 19, 1865.
Miller, Ira, aged 75.
Miller, George R., " Nov. —, 18—.
Miller, Willard, (died at Durham) Dec. 17, 1870. .
Miller, Henry L., age 59, died April 24, 1874.
Nichols, Sylvanus' child, (still-born) July 11, 1791.
Nichols, Sylvanus' child, died Dec. 11, 1793.
Nichols, Sylvanus' wife, died Oct. 17, 1821.
Norton, Mary, wife of James, age 27, died Mar. 2, 1844.
Nichols, Sylvanus, age 90, died Oct. 14, 1849.
North, Delia, wife of Charles, and daughter of N.
    Warner.
Nichols, Sylvanus, age 58, died March 1, 1859.
Parsons, Stephen's wife, " Feb. 11, 1777.
Parsons, Stephen's 2d wife, " Sept. 29, 1781.
Paine, Widow, " July 3, 1786.
Parsons, Aaron, " July 28, 1791.
Pomp, old blind Slave of Abel Birdsey, 1831.
Phillis, wid. of Peter (col.), once slave of Dr. Rawson,
    age 82, died Oct. 16, 1836.
Prout, Eliza, wife of Sylvester.
Prout, Mary, daughter of Sylvester.
Potter, Francis' wife.
Potter, Francis' 2d wife.
Ranney, Rhoda, died Jan. 11, 1772.
Roberts, Noah's child, died Feb. 10, 1774.
Roberts, David's child, " Sept. 3, 1776.
Rockwell, John, " Jan. 18, 1780.
Rockwell, Phebe, wid., " Dec. 14, 1782.
Rockwell, Joshua's child, drowned June 28, 1790.
Roberts, David, Jun.'s wife, died Dec. 15, 1793.
Roberts, Nathan's child, " Jan. 31, 1795.
Ranney, Hannah, " Mar. 30, 1798.
Roberts, David's wife, " May 23, 1802.
Richardson, Mrs., " July 29, 1811.

Rich, Bathsheba.
Roberts, David,   died Nov. 15, 1818.
Roberts, Ami's wife, "   1820.
Roberts, Ami's child, "   Sept., 1821.
Roberts, Ami,   "   Feb. 24, 1843.
Rice, Hezekiah,   "   1852.
Ross, Abraham's child.
Ross, Adam's wife, died 1855.
Rice, Lydia, wid of Hezekiah R., age 96, died 1861.
Stow, Dan (fit—frozen), died Jan. 16, 1770.
Spencer, Himor's child, "   Jan. 20, 1770.
Scovel, Elizabeth,   "   Nov. 11, 1781.
Squires, John,   "   Jan. 18, 1782.
Squires, John's widow, "   Feb. 7, 1783.
Smith's child,   "   Feb. 29, 1784.
Stocking, Martha, widow, "   Nov. 13, 1790.
Stocker, Mary, widow, "   Nov. 22, 1793.
Stow, Eliakim,   "   1797.
Stow, Obed's wife Anna, age 32, died Nov. 23, 1802.
Stevens, Robert, died Nov. 13, 1803.
Stow, Jemima, wife of Elihu S., died Oct. 12, 1805.
Sexton, Jonathan's wife,   "   July 1, 1806.
Spencer, Elihu's child,   "   Jan. 20, 1807.
Stow, Elihu,   "   Nov. 13, 1812.
Stow, William, son of Obed, "   Nov. 11, 1814.
Strong, Widow, of Durham.
Sizer, Comfort, son of Lot S., age 15, died March, 1816.
Spencer, Elihu, age over 70, died Sept. 16, 1820.
Stow, Zaccheus' wife, died Oct. 26, 1821.
Skinner, Nancy, wife of Horace, age 33, died Aug. 10,
       1828.   [The 2d grave in the new ground for her.]
Stow, Albert G., age 28, died (at Stow, Ohio), Feb.
       25, 1829.
Spencer, Diadema, died Jan. 15, 1831.
Stow, Eunice,   "   May 21, 1838.
Stow, Elihu, age 78, "   April 19, 1830.

Stow, Delia, age 26, daughter of Warren P., died Aug. 2, 1839.

Stow, Obed, age 72 (interred in old burying-ground), died Sept. 5, 1839.

Stow, Joshua (Judge), age 80, died Oct. 10, 1842.

Spencer, Lucy, wife of Ezra.   "   Feb. 21, 1845.

Spencer, Delia Ann, age 14.   "   May 6, 1845.

Spencer, Samuel's child,   "   Jan. 30, 1842.

Stow, Lucy, wid. of Obed,   "   April 10, 1853.

Stow, Ruth, wid. of Judge S., age 90, died Feb. 23, 1852.

Stow, Mary, wid. of Elihu (at Granville, Mass.), 1853.

Stow, Warren P., age 63, died April 5, 1856.

Skinner, Horace, Dea., age 54, died Oct. 4, 1848.

Stevens, Mary, died (at Capt. David Birdsey's place) May 20, 1858.

Skinner, Elvina. died (of consumption) March 8, 1859.

Smith, John, aged 70, died Nov. 18, 1859.

Skinner, Emily, died (of consumption) Sept. 22, 1860.

Starr, Matilda, wife of Luther, age 70 (of cancer), 1861.

Stow, E. W., wid. of W. P. Stow, age 85, died Feb. 5, 1877.

Turner, Jonathan's child, died Feb. 16, 1763.

Turner, John, son of Stephen, died Mar. 13, 1764.

Turner, Jonathan's wife,   "   July 29, 1766.

Topping, Joseph's child,   "   June 4, 1779.

Turner, Stephen,   "   May 5, 1780.

Topping, Elias,   "   April 17, 1781.

Turner, Hannah, wid.,   "   May 16, 1790.

Turner, Joel's child,   "   Oct. 25, 1800.

Truby, Mrs.,   "   Oct. 8, 1802.

Turner, Stephen's, Capt., child, (still-born) June 12, 1803.

Turner, Stephen, Capt., died Aug. 10, 1804.

Turner, Elizabeth, w. of Stephen, died Aug. 13, 1804.

Turner, Edward's child, died Nov. 22, 1807.

11

Turner, Jonathan, died Jan. 9, 1811.

Turner, Eunice, wid. of Jonathan, died July 6, 1811.

Turner, Edward's child, 6 mos. old, died Sept. 17, 1818.

Toals, wife of Amos, died Oct. 10, 1813.

Turner, Edward's child, 11 hours old, Feb. 28, 1819.

Turner, Edward's child, died Jan. 16, 1820.

Turner, Emory, age 20,   "   Jan. 8, 1824.

Turner, Edward's child, 3 mos. old, Aug. 4, 1827.

Thomas, Susan, age 15, died Nov. 26, 1827.

Turner, Theron, son of John, died Dec. 31, 1842.

Thomas, Marvin, age 48, died (heart disease) Oct. 3, 1853.

Thomas, Lucretia, wid. of Marvin T.

Wetmore, Beriah, Jun.'s child, died Feb. 10, 1764.

Wetmore, Beriah, Jun.'s 2d child, " Jan. 28, 1765.

Wetmore, David's child,   "   June 17, 1766.

Wetmore, Dorothy,   "   Nov. 26, 1769.

Ward, William's wife,   "   Dec. 25, 1770.

Wetmore, Hope's child,   "   April 4, 1772.

Warner, Samuel, Jun.'s child, (still-born) Feb. 16, 1773.

Warner, Samuel, Capt., died Sept. 3, 1773.

Wetmore Samuel (of Winchester), died Dec. 30, 1773.

White, Jedediah's child, died Feb. 8, 1774.

Wetmore, David, died at Litchfield, June 15, 1774.

Ward, William, Jun.'s child, died Dec. 22, 1775.

Wetmore, Thomas' wife,   "   April 13, 1776.

Wetmore, Thomas,   "   April 23, 1776.

Wetmore, Nathaniel, son of Joseph, died July 23, 1776.

Wetmore, Amos, Capt.'s child,   "   Aug. 19, 1779.

Wetmore, Ethan's child,   "   Dec. 14, 1779.

Wetmore, Capt. Caleb's wife,   "   Feb. 7, 1783.

Wetmore, Joseph, died June 23, 1783.

Walker, James' child, (still-born) Oct. 17, 1783.

Ward, William, Capt., died Feb. 25, 1786.

Ward, Dr. Asher's child, "   June 10, 1786.

Wetmore, Ethan's child, died Dec. 14, 1779.

Wetmore, Capt. Caleb, died March 4, 1788.
Ward, Dr. Asher,   "   Aug. 22, 1788.
Washburn, Joseph's child, died Aug. 28, 1788.
Wetmore, Sarah, age 29,   "   Aug. 16, 1791.
Wetmore, Polly, or Mary, age 22, daughter of John,
    died Dec. 10, 1792.
Wetmore, Ethan, died Dec. 14, 1792.
Ward, Timothy,   "   Jan. 7, 1793.
Wetmore, Lois,   "   Jan. 24, 1794.
Wetmore, Jesse's child, died Jan. 31, 1794.
Ward, William, Jun.,   "   April 18, 1795.
Webster, Widow,   "   Jan. 25, 1795.
Wetmore, Jesse's child,   "   Jan. 31, 1795.
Ward, James' child,   "   Oct. 2, 1797.
Walker, James' child,   "   Jan. 31, 1798.
Wetmore, Jesse's child,   "   May 22, 1801.
Wetmore, Jesse's 3d child,"   June 12, 1801.
Ward, Sylvester's child,   "   July 18, 1804.
Ward, Comfort, died (in Carolina) Oct. 27, 1806.
Wetmore, Francis, died Sept. 9, 1807.
Wetmore, Bela,   "   May 5, 1809.
Wetmore, Daniel's wife, died Sept. 14, 1813.
Wetmore, Joseph,   "   Aug. 19, 1814.
Ward, Irena, daughter of James, died Nov. 20, 1814.
Ward, Sylvester's child (son),   "   Sept. 11, 1815.
Wetmore, Daniel, age 91.   "   Jan., 1817.
Ward, Mary, wife of William W., age 71, died Oct. 15,
    1817.
Ward, William, age 75, died Nov. 26, 1819.
Wetherell, Simeon's child, (drowned) June 26, 1820.
Wright, Eliza, age 26, wife of Horace (paper-maker),
    died Oct. 31, 1825.
Ward, James, age 55, died Sept. 9, 182-.
White, Benjamin,   "   May, 182-.
Ward, Elizabeth, age 24, died (consumption) Jan., 183-.
Ward, Capt. James T., age 88, died April 9, 183-.

It is probable that most of those who died in Middlefield before a common burial ground was selected were interred in the First Society. As our record does not go back to the time of the first burial in the yard by 23 years, this desideratum in part has been supplied by copying from some of the old moss-grown gravestones. This record of the deaths in Middlefield was kept by Hezekiah Hale (sexton) from 1761 till January, 1814, and then by Joshua Stow till near the time of his death, Oct. 10, 1842. Since his death the record has been irregularly kept and is very imperfect. As the "Graveyard" in Middlefield was not laid out till the year 1737, the dead previous to this, must have been interred in the First Society within the limits of the city of Middletown, for the first settlers came from said Society. Allowing the settlement of Middlefield to have occurred in 1700, there would be a period of 37 years before the "North Graveyard" was made a place of sepulture. The first grave dug in this yard was for Hannah Turner, wife of Stephen Turner, in 1738, as marked on the gravestone.

Samuel Wetmore, first settler, died in 1746, age 91 years.

John Chilson died 1747.

Jonathan Dowd died in 1745.

Benjamin Miller, first settler, died in 1747, age 76 years.

Abraham Turner's wife died 1750.

Naomi Parsons died 1753.

Mercy Miller, wid. of Benjamin, died 1756.
David Gould died 1756.

HOUSEHOLDERS IN MIDDLETOWN IN 1670, TWENTY
YEARS AFTER THE FIRST SETTLEMENT OF
FIFTEEN FAMILIES IN 1650.

Allen, Thomas.
Allen, Obadiah.
Bacon, Nathaniel.
Briggs, William.
Bow, Alexander.
Cornwell, William.
Cornwell, John.
Cornwell, Samuel.
Cornwell, William, Jr.
Collins, Nathaniel.
Collins, Samuel.
Call, Honory.
Clements, Jeffreys.
Cheney, William.
Durant, George.
Eggleston, Samuel.
Foster, Edward.
Hubbard, Joseph.
Hubbard, Daniel.
Hubbard, Thomas.
Harris, Daniel.
Harris, William.
Hall, John.
Hall, Richard.
Hall, John, Jr.
Hall, Samuel.

Hamlin, Giles.
Hubbard, George.
Johnson, Isaac.
Kirby, John.
Lucas, William.
Lane, Isaac.
Miller, Thomas.
Martin, Anthony.
Ranny, Thomas.
Savage, John.
Stocking, Samuel.
Stow, Samuel.
Stow, Thomas.
Stow, John.
Sage, David.
Tappan, James.
Turner, Edward.
Wetmore, Thomas.
Wilcox, Thomas.
Wilcox, John.
Ward, John.
Ward, William.
Warner, Andrew.
Warner, Robert.
Warner, John.
White, Thomas.

11*

Of the first settlers, the Bacon, Hall, and Cornwell families were direct from England. Sage and Wetmore from Wales. Ranny from Scotland. Hubbard, Wilcox, Lucas, Warner, and Allen from Hartford and Windsor, Conn. Kerby, Harris, from Boston. Miller and Ward from Rowley, Mass. Stow from Concord, Mass. Johnson from Roxbury.

CENSUS OF

MIDDLEFIELD BY SCHOOL DISTRICTS,

SEPTEMBER, 1848.

EAST SCHOOL DISTRICT.

	Fam.	Pop.		Fam.	Pop.
Smith Birdsey,	1	4	Amos Miller & Mary,	2	6
Amos Coe,	1	5	George R. Miller,	1	4
Benjamin Miller,	1	2	Ira Miller,	1	5
Hiram Miller,	1	5	Charles Hubbard,	1	8
Elisha Miller,	1	3	Roswell Lee,	1	5
Benjamin Coe,	1	4	Elisha Bailey,	1	5
Hiram Birdsey,	1	3	Horace Walmsley		
Daniel H. Birdsey,	1	4	(col.),	1	3
Samuel Birdsey,	1	2	Cornelius Hall,	1	6
Alvin Birdsey,	1	4	Lucy Coe, widow,	1	4
Curtis Coe,	1	5			

SOUTH SCHOOL DISTRICT.

	Fam.	Pop.		Fam.	Pop.
John Birdsey,	1	6	Sally Cook, widow,	1	1
William Lyman,	1	11	Isaac Coe,	1	3
Edwin Skinner,	1	3	Rev. James More,	1	5
Marvin Thomas,	1	3	Andrew Coe,	1	7
Horace Skinner,	1	10	Eunice Ward, wid.,	1	3
Enoch Coe,	1	5	Electa Boardman,	1	3
Elbert Miller,	1	5	Mrs. Skinner,	1	1
James Thrall,	1	6	Mary Lucas, widow,	1	2

	Fam.	Pop.		Fam.	Pop.
James Norton,	1	7	Olmstead Brainerd,	1	4
Eben Coe,	1	4	Abigail Miller, wid.,	1	4
Lois Coe, widow,	1	3	Roswell Bailey,	1	5
Nelson Coe,	1	9	Jeremiah Miller,	1	4
Elias C. Coe,	1	4	William P. Abel,	1	5
William W. Coe,	1	6	Isaac Miller,	1	3
Albert Skinner,	1	6	Sylvester Mills,	1	2
Elbert Coe,	1	5	Russell Bailey,	1	5

NORTH SCHOOL DISTRICT.

	Fam.	Pop.		Fam.	Pop.
George Bacon,	1	5	Polly Coe, widow,	1	1
Capt. Joseph Coe,	1	2	Sylvester Prout,	1	5
Roswell Hale and			Phineas M. Angur,	1	3
Mother,	1	2	Sylvanus Nichols,	1	4
Ichabod Miller,	1	5	Calvin Hall,	1	3
Jesse Miller and			Hiram Hall,	1	3
Mother,	1	5	Horace Roberts,	1	6
Amelia Coe,	1	3	Lois Roberts,	1	1
Luther Coe,	1	4	Levi Coe, Col.,	1	3
Harley Hall,	1	6	David B. Miller,	1	9
Miles Hall,	1	10	John Williams,	1	5
Wid. Cook (toll-gate),	1	2	Nelson Miller,	1	4
Amos Williams,	1	2	Joshua Miller,	1	2
Capt. John Bacon			AugustusCarter(col.),	1	4
and O. Foster,	1	5	Lucy Stow, widow,	1	3
Cornelia Johnson and			Anna Skinner,	1	3
sister,	1	4	Sabrina Geer, widow,	1	5
Sanford Coe,	1	5	George W. Miller,		3
Wilson Cook,	1	4	Polly Angur,	1	1

FALLS SCHOOL DISTRICT.
"PAPER-MILL QUARTER," AS FIRST CALLED.

	Fam.	Pop.		Fam.	Pop.
Augustus Burnham,	1	5	Warren Coles,	1	6
Sherman Hubbard,	1	3	James Mulvany,	1	8

	Fam.	Pop.		Fam.	Pop.
Luther Starr,	1	3	Josiah Walmsley, (col.)	1	3
Simeon Wetherill,	1	9	John Dickinson,	1	4
Stephen Grace,	1	4	John Lucas,	1	3
John Ferry,	1	6	Thomas Atkins,	1	6
Abraham Warner and			Harrison Bates,		2
David,	1	7	Asher Miller,	1	8
John North,	1	4	Asa Kimball,	1	7
Nelson Aston,	1	2	Lewis Miller,	1	3
Ira N. Johnson,	1	7	Harvey Miller,	1	3
Peter Ashton,	1	5	Sylvester C. Bailey,	1	9
Sibyl Aston, widow,	1	4	Mary Weir,	1	11
Freeman Johnson,	1	5	Josiah Benton,	1	2
Phineas W. Birdsey,	1	5	Richard M. Bailey,	1	4
Eunice Ives, widow,	1	2	Richard Russell,	1	8
Eliza Daniels,	1	4	James Smith,	1	3
Chester Atkins,	1	2	Jared Grover,	1	4
John Ross,	1	3			

MIDDLEFIELD GRAND LEVY, A. D. 1747.

Allen, Samuel (one of first settlers),	£63	9s.
Birdsey, John,	119	11
Bartlett, John,	112	10
Bacon, Nathaniel,	80	18
Bacon, Joseph,	38	2
Coe, Joseph, Jr.,	104	5
Chilson, John, Jr.,	29	16
Camp, Abraham,	63	12
Coe, Ephraim,	6	10
Coe, David,	83	10
Camp, Edward,	86	1
Cook, Jacob,	31	0
Coe, Robert,	94	18
Coe, Joseph, Capt.,	9	7
Chilson, John,	66	5
Deaming, Jeremiah,	33	16
Dowd, Jacob,	42	12
Hubbard, Ebenezer,	64	6
Hale, Joseph,	71	0
Hale, Ebenezer, Jr.,	26	6
Lyman, John,	91	7
Lyman, Noah,	12	2
Lane, Elizabeth,	5	0
Leaming, Matthias,	50	15
Miller, Benjamin (one of first settlers),	164	4

Miller, Benjamin, Jr.,	£102	9s.
Miller, Joseph,	123	6
Miller, Giles,	25	8
Miller, Joseph, Jr.,	31	10
Miller, Amos,	109	0
Miller, David,	85	11
Miller, Ichabod,	112	0
Parsons, Aaron,	93	10
Parsons, Moses,	107	8
Parsons, Simeon,	8	8
Parsons, Ithamar,	11	14
Parsons, Timothy,	12	18
Parsons, Moses, Sr.,	13	16
Rockwell, John,	49	0
Strickland, David,	41	10
Sheldon, Moses,	41	0
Stow, Hawley Samuel,	31	12
Stevenson, Amasa,	18	0
Stow, Eliakim,	92	18
Stow, Daniel,	36	2
Talcot, John,	98	0
Turner, Stephen,	81	18
Tibbals, Joseph,	3	2
Talcot, Hezekiah,	17	4
Wetmore, Joseph,	75	8
Ward, William, Jr.,	45	18
Wetmore, Samuel (one of first settlers),	104	7
Wetmore, Fitz John,	18	0
Wetmore, Benjamin,	33	0
Warner, Samuel, Lieut.,	111	6

Wetmore, Hezekiah, Jr.,	.	.	£18	0s.
Wetmore, Caleb,	.	.	72	0
Wetmore, Hope,	.	.	6	13
Wetmore, Samuel, Jr.,	.	.	24	0
Wales, Nathaniel,	.	.	32	12
Wetmore, Beriah, Jr.,	.	.	18	0
Wetmore, Dorothy, .	.	.	25	16

	AGE.		AGE.
†Mrs. Ross, widow,	91	*Warren Coles,	74
*Sibyl Aston, widow,	82	*Elias C. Coe,	88
*Curtis Coe,	89	†Mrs. Elias Coe,	87
*John Dickinson,	89	*Mrs. Eli Coe,	86
*Mrs. Hale, widow,	89	*Mrs. A. Bailey, wid.,	82
*Richard M. Bailey,	78	†Mrs. A. Rockwell,	75
*Thomas Atkins,	78	†Mrs. D. Coe, wid.,	75
Mr. Fagan,	77	Mrs. W. Skinner, wid.,	80
*Mrs. W. Lyman, wid.,	89	†Miss Almira Ward,	78
†Col. Amos Miller,	79	*Miss Laura Darrow,	86
†Mrs. Ira Miller, wid.,	80	*Sylvester Hall,	78
*Miss Harriet Miller,	78	Mrs. S. Nichols,	80
*Mrs. John Birdsey,	86	Mrs. Benj. Miller,	81
Patrick Dooley,	75	*Miles Hall,	74
Mrs. Dooley,	75	*Mrs. W.P. Stow, wid.,	81
*Hiram Miller,	76		

At this time there were more old people in this town than at any other time since its settlement.

[Those marked thus * known to have died before August, 1883; those marked thus † known to be living at that time.]

12

HISTORY OF LONG HILL.

Long Hill lies south of the city of Middletown, Conn., and is three miles and ten rods long,
and one mile and two hundred and twenty-seven
rods wide, and contains about 3,656 square acres.
Bounded, north, partly on the city line of Middletown, and partly on Staddle Hill; east, on the
Farm Hill district; south, on Durham line, and
West on the line of Middlefield. This estimate
is for Long Hill proper, or before the Durant
District was formed. More territory was taken
in the formation of this district from the East
District than from the West. Previous to this the
two districts were nearly equally divided. Now
the West District has about 2,070 acres, whereas
the East District has not far from 1,590 acres.
This estimate is predicated on the late county
map. An actual survey might vary it some, but it
is deemed near enough for all practical purposes.
Highways and ponds are included in this estimate. Long Hill took its name from the succes-
sion of hills that begin to rise near the center
and extend south to the Durham line. This is
Dr. Field's opinion. Some have supposed that
it took its name from the high hill near the center
of the place.

THE FACE OF THE COUNTRY OF THESE DISTRICTS.

Most of Long Hill is well adapted to farming purposes. The early settlers had a great deal of heavy work in clearing off the stones, as the old moss-covered walls will show. Nearly enough stones were found to fence the land, on its surface. The stones were generally sandstone, and in some places there were large boulders. These were cut and used for cellar walls; they were generally too coarse for hewing. The "Wall Rocks," lying in the south part of the East District are a conglomeration of sand and pebbles of white, and blue, and red, and most of these rocks are too coarse and flinty for building purposes. In the south part of Long Hill, in both districts, are beautiful groves of chestnut and other timber, much of which is the second growth. Some of this timber land is rocky and unfit for cultivation, but well adapted to the growth of forests. The hills in the south part and near the Durham line, are the highest hills in Middletown. The sight from Round Hill is grand; from this hill in clear weather, can be seen Mounts Tom and Holyoke in Mass., with the naked eye. The scenery from "Long Hill" near the center of this place, is delightful. This hill, rising out of a valley and lying equidistant from Besek or Meriden Mt. on the West, and Cobalt Mt. and White Rocks on the East, and the surrounding towns and the winding Connecticut River, all lend enchantment to this lovely place.

THE SETTLEMENT OF LONG HILL WAS NEAR 1675.

The first settlers in Long Hill were the Halls. They spread out from the First Society. Soon other settlers followed. The Hubbards, the Clarks, the Crowells, and families by the name of Atkins, Barnes, Ward, and Blake. Most of these families settled on parcels of land regularly laid out. These several pieces of land were laid out, north and south from sixty to eighty rods wide, and extended to the Durham line. The westernmost tract was taken by the Barnes families, and was eight rods wide, extending to the Durham line. The west tract was taken by the Crowells and others. The next by the Hubbards and the Atkins. This bordered on the old Durham road; then east of this was the Clark tract of land, he being the sole owner. This piece was eighty rods wide, and extended south to the Durham line. The next tract of land, east, was settled by Wards and Blakes; and still further east there were Wards and Crowells. All the several tracts of land were bounded north by the east and west highway, on which stood the stone school-houses. A more particular history of these first families will be given under their proper heads.

CHARACTERISTICS OF THE FIRST SETTLERS.

The first settlers were athletic, substantial men and women. The Hubbards were noted for being spry and active. Jumping and wrestling were much practiced in the early history of this place. Ball playing in the spring, especially at election days, and the pitching of quoits was much attended to, at odd spells. The Crowells were stout, tall, robust men, could lift and carry heavy burdens; men well calculated to clear up and subdue this hard and stony soil. The Halls were stout, strong, intellectual people. There are amongst the old deeds and papers in the family of a descendant of Calvin Hall (Deacon Stephen's), some that date back to 1698. A deed of land from John Hall, ensign, and wife to their son John Hall. Also a military commission, among these old papers, conferring on John Hall a Captain's commission, in the reign of King William, styled "King of England, Scotland, France, and Ireland," signed by John Winthrop, Governor of the colonies of Connecticut. This commission dates back to 1699. There were other papers of ancient date, some in the reign of Queen Anne.

JOHN HALL.

John Hall, Jun., from the best accounts, was the first settler in Long Hill. His house stood a little north of the brook and the stone quarries, on the road west of the Pameachy Pond, and was built not far from the year 1698. (The old

12*

house was taken down by Calvin Hall, grandson of Daniel Hall, in the year 1822, and a new one built in its place.) When the Indians became less troublesome, and less formidable, the whites spread out into the country around the first settlement. Long Hill, most of it, was a dense forest with, here and there, a small patch cleared off by the Indians, where they raised their corn. Wolves and bears roamed at leisure through these forests, and over these fields that are now smiling in beauty. under the hand of civilization.

JACOB HALL.

Jacob Hall, a son of John Hall, built a house, south from Trench Hill, in a commanding place on the west bank of the Pameachy, wherein he lived and died. He was brother of Calvin Hall. His children were :

Leonard,	Jacob, 2d,
Henry,	Daughters —

Jacob died at the South. Henry Hall occupied the old homestead, and in 1879, at the time of this record, was eighty-four years old. He beautified the old place: painted the old house white, which was previously red, and the house was as a "house standing on a hill which cannot be hid."

JOHN HALL 2D.

John Hall 2d, an early settler in Long Hill. His house stood on the old Durham road, about one mile south of the city of Middletown. He married Esther Hubbard (daughter of Nathaniel Hubbard and Sarah Johnson). John Hall's house was built about the year 1753. The house was taken down in the year 18—, and a brick house built in place of the old one by W. Steuben, who married Sarah Crowell, a grand-daughter of John Hall. The children of John and Esther Hubbard Hall were, sons:

David, John, and Jonathan.

Daughters:

Elizabeth, who married a Miller.

Esther, unmarried.

Phebe, who married a Ward.

Ruth, who married a Starr, and

Sarah, who married S. Crowell.

AMBROSE CLARK.

Ambrose Clark was one of the earliest settlers of Long Hill. He was called "Lord Am.," on account of his being so great a landholder. His tract of land, east of the Hubbard tract, was eighty rods wide, extending south to the Durham line. He built his house on the hill north, and near the center of his land on the East and West Road. His house was erected not far from the year 1720. It was built somewhat in the manner and form of the "Captain Wait Cornwell house" (the oldest house in Long Hill), except, there was no "lintel" roof. The house was forty-two feet long and twenty-two feet wide, and two stories high, with a stone chimney near the center of the house ten feet square or more. The posts were eighteen inches square above the first story. The beams through the center were twelve by sixteen inches square, and all of oak. The clapboards were of rived oak. There was no plaster on any of the rooms. The joists over-head were planed and beaded, and the walls below were sealed with pitch pine. The house was occupied as a dwelling-house some eighty or ninety years. The last occupant was William Miller, who married a daughter of Clark. He sold out the homestead to Ithamar Atkins and moved to Middlefield. Atkins turned this for-midable and antique building into a barn, by taking out the chimney which made plenty of room, and sufficiently high to admit a load of hay. The parlor was turned into stables for calves, sheep, and colts. The place, where was once mirth and beauty, dancing, and feasting, became the quiet abode of a lower order of animals. What a change! In the orchard adjoining the house was once a marriage feast. Betsey Higgins was the bride, and the groom was James Beers. It seems that the bride's parents were opposed to the match; as a consequence she was married out in the orchard. There was a gen-eral invitation given out and many availed them-selves of the unusual circumstance. The marriage ceremony was performed by Parson Enoch Hunt-ington, then a young man in the ministry. The bride selected the following hymn, which was

sung to the displeasure of some, and the delight
of many. It can be found in Dwight's collection
of Psalms and Hymns, published in 1808 :

> Thou God of love, Thou ever blest,
>   Pity my suffering state.
> When wilt thou set my soul at rest
>   From lips that love deceit?
>
> Hard lot of mine, my days are cast
>   Among the sons of strife,
> Whose never ceasing brawlings waste
>   My golden hours of life.
>
> O, might I fly to change my place,
>   How would I choose to dwell
> In some wide, lonesome wilderness,
>   And leave these gates of hell!
>
> Peace is the blessing that I seek,
>   How lovely are its charms.
> I am for peace, but when I speak
>   They all declare for arms.
>
> New passions fill their souls, engage
>   And keep their malice strong.
> What shall be done to curb thy rage?
>   O, thou devouring tongue!

The cake was carried around in a corn basket!
no plates were used. There are none now living
that attended this strange wedding, and very
few living who heard those speak of the event
who were eye-witnesses of the novel scene.
Ninety years and more in sublunary things!
The house, the barn are gone ; the apples trees
are gone, where youth and beauty met and shook
hands. All are gone !

NATHANIEL HUBBARD.

Nathaniel Hubbard, one of the early settlers in Long Hill (about the year 1715), was the son of Nathaniel the first, of Middletown, and Mary Earl (born Dec. 10, 1652). He was the youngest son of George Hubbard, who was born at Wakefield, England, in 1594, and who came to Hartford, Conn., in 1636, and in 1640 married Elizabeth Watts, daughter of Richard Watts. He left Hartford in 1650, and settled in Middletown, where he died March 18, 1685. Nathaniel Hubbard's house stood on the cross road, east and west, a little north of the brick house built by his son Noadiah in the year 1787. The house stood on the east side of the road (as it now is), nearly where the barn now stands; the old barn stood on the opposite side of the road, and here it may be well to notice that the old Durham road was laid out due north and south, and met the cross road near the old stone school-house; then the traveling public had to turn a sharp angle down the hill to the road leading to the new city of Middletown. So, in reality, all the first houses in this vicinity were built on the original highways. This road was laid out more than 100 years ago. It commenced south of the brick house built by Ithamar Atkins, crossed the Atkins farm, and through the Hubbard home lot, between the house and barn, to the highway. This road shortened the distance, a steep hill was avoided, and travelers much benefited. The children of Nathaniel Hubbard and Sarah Johnson were:

Nathaniel,   Samuel.
Nehemiah,   Noadiah.

Nehemiah was born July 22, 1721. The daughters were Esther, who married John Hall, 2d daughter married a Lawson, 3d married a Warner. But two of the children of Nathaniel settled in Long Hill permanently, namely, Nehemiah and Noadiah.

NEHEMIAH HUBBARD.

Nehemiah, the second son of Nathaniel and grandson of Nathaniel the first, of Middletown, Conn. (who was born Dec. 10, 1652, and who was the youngest son of George Hubbard, who was born at Wakefield, England, in 1594, and who came to Hartford, Conn., in 1636, and in 1640 married Elizabeth Watts, daughter of Richard Watts. He left Hartford in 1650, and settled in Middletown, Conn., where he died March 18, 1685).

Nehemiah Hubbard married Sarah Sill, daughter of Joseph Sill and Phebe Lord, of Lyme, Conn. Their children were:

Isaac, b. Sept. 24, 1749, m. R. Coleman.
Nehemiah, b. April 10, 1752, m. 1, C. Willis, 2, L. Starr, 3, — Latimer.
Elisha, b. Oct. 1, 1753, m. M. Roberts.
Lucy, b. April 22, 1755, m. Rev. R. Hubbard.
David, b. Feb. 24, 1757, d. unmarried.

Jacob, b. Jan. 28, 1759, m. 1, S. Hobby, 2, S. Hall.

Sarah, b. Jan. 16,   , m. Daniel Crowell.

Phebe, b. Jan. 3,   , m. Elijah Roberts.

Anna, b. Oct. 18, 1762, m. Ithamar Atkins.

Mary, b. Aug. 18, 1764, d. in childhood.

Mary 2d, b. Aug. 20, 1765, m. G. Lyman.

Nathaniel, b. July 17, 1766, lost at sea.

Matthew, b. Nov. 20, 1770, d. in childhood.

Nehemiah Hubbard bought a piece of land on the corner of Middlefield and Laurel Grove streets, in the year 1744, and soon after erected a house on the corner of the lot. (The house is now standing and in good repair, after a lapse of more than 135 years.) He was a very cheerful man, and cheerfulness is conducive to old age. He was 93 years old when he died. When he was 84 years old he went down in his well on the stones and got a pail of milk which had fallen into the well. When at an advanced age in life he used to go to church on horseback, carrying his wife behind him on a pillion. He took great interest in schools, as well as in church matters. He visited some of the schools when he was over 80 years old, and spoke encouraging words to the children. The writer of this memoir remembers a visit the good old man made at the "Old Stone School-house" in 1805 or 1806. In his remarks he adverted to the Revolutionary war, and told the children the cost of freedom. He had at one time six sons in the war. One thing in regard to Sarah, the wife of Nehemiah Hubbard, may seem strange and inexplicable to many, but it must be true, or at least an uncommon work of the imagination. She was sitting alone in a pew in the old Congregational church on High street, Middletown, near where the college buildings of the Wesleyan University now stand. She had taken her seat early in the afternoon : there were few, if any, in the church beside herself. While sitting there in meditation, she turned her head toward the door and saw her son Nathaniel, in sailors' costume, coming up the aisle toward her. As he approached her, she reached out her arms to embrace him, when he vanished from her sight. At that time her son, being on a sea voyage, was blown off from the topmast while furling the sail in a fierce gale of wind, and drowned near the coast of Ireland. He appeared to his mother at the exact time of his death, as she learned when the vessel came back into port. Now, this woman was the grandmother of the writer of this history, and was not a believer in witchcraft, or in any supernatural things, although such beliefs were prevalent at this time in many towns in New England.

ELISHA HUBBARD.

Elisha, the third son of Nehemiah first, married Martha Roberts. He settled at the old homestead of his father. Their children were :

13

Elisha the 2d, b. 1792.

Martha, b. June 20, 1794.

Rebecca, b. Dec. 1, 1795.

Ann, b. April 23, 1797.

Sarah, b. June   , 1799.

Phebe, b. Feb. 10, 1801.

An infant child died between the births of Phebe and Daniel.

Daniel, b. Oct. 21, 1803.

David, b. Sept. 28, 1805.

Mary, the youngest, b. Feb. 23, 1808.

In his youthful days, Elisha Hubbard was very spry. Six hogsheads, with one head out of each, were placed in a row, and he could jump from the ground into the first one, and then out and in through the whole six without faltering. He was early in the Revolutionary war; was taken prisoner at Fort Washington, and confined in the Sugar House, New York city. After some time he was exchanged, came home and got recruited, and then enlisted for the remainder of the war.

While a prisoner in the Sugar House, a comrade of Elisha's, not quite dead, was being dragged down the stairs and out of the prison by a British officer; Elisha, indignant and daring, rushed after to rescue his dying comrade, and narrowly escaped being run through by the bayonet. The Hubbards were intrepid, cool, not counting danger until it was past. In private life they were always to be relied upon for doing

things that required steady nerves and physical
courage.

In 1878, September 11th, there was a family
gathering at the old homestead built by Nehemiah Hubbard, and the six sisters, grandchildren
of Nehemiah and daughters of Elisha were all
there under the paternal roof where they were
born.

NEHEMIAH HUBBARD 2D.

Nehemiah, second son of Nehemiah the first,
was born April 10, 1752. The following sketch
of his life is copied from an obituary notice in
the "Sentinel and Witness" of Middletown,
Conn., February 15, 1837: "At the age of 14 he
went to live with Col. Matthew Talcott as clerk
in his store, where he continued until he was 21
years of age. Early in 1776 he entered the
army, and in May of that year he was appointed
by Gov. Trumbull paymaster of the regiment
commanded by Col. Burrall, and which was sent
on service to the shore of Lake Champlain. He
first went and paid the troops at Forts Stanwix,
Schuyler, and Herkimer, on the Mohawk, and
then joined his regiment at Fort Ticonderoga,
where he remained some time. In May, 1777,
he was appointed by Major-General Greene—who
was at that time Quartermaster-General of the
United States—his deputy for the State of Connecticut, which post he filled until the resignation
of Gen. Greene. He was again appointed by Col.
Pickering, then acting as Quartermaster-General,

but he declined. He continued, however, to discharge the duties of Deputy Quartermaster-General until relieved by another person, when he entered into the service with Wadsworth & Carter, who supplied the French army. This he accompanied to Yorktown, and was present at the surrender of Lord Cornwallis. As a provider of public supplies, all his movements were marked by decision, promptness, and punctuality. The resources of Connecticut were brought forward at the most critical juncture, and while the army was enduring the greatest privations it was frequently relieved by this State through his energy and extraordinary exertions. As a specimen of the confidence reposed in him by such men as Washington, Greene, Trumbull, and Hamilton, it ought to be mentioned that after the organization of the present Government, Col. Hamilton, while Secretary of the Treasury, was pressingly urgent to have him take the management of an institution which he wished to establish for promoting the manufactures of the country. After the close of the Revolution he settled in Middletown, Conn., as a merchant, where he continued the remainder of his life. He was President of the Middletown Bank from 1808 to 1822, when he resigned, being 70 years of age. He was also first President of the Savings Bank, and held that place until his death. Many instances have come to the knowledge of the writer in which he showed the most enlarged liberality in furnishing young men and other persons with money to enable them to begin and advance in business. In person Mr. Hubbard was rather above the ordinary stature, his appearance commanding, and he retained an erect form until the last, with an uncommon exemption from most of the infirmities of age. As a man of business he was uncommonly methodical, and was altogether one of the first merchants of his day. In his private walk and character were beheld all the stern virtues that adorned the lives of some of the best of the New England Pilgrim Fathers. He died February 6, 1837, aged 85 years. Many of his ancestors and relatives were distinguished for longevity.

ROBERT HUBBARD.

Robert Hubbard, one of the early settlers of East Long Hill, settled about the year 1730. He married Elizabeth Sill, the second daughter of Joseph Sill and Phebe Lord, of Lyme, Conn., Oct. 9, 1735. He was the son of Robert Hubbard and Abigail Atkins, and born at Middletown, 1673, and grandson of George Hubbard, who was born in Wakefield, England, 1594. and who came to Hartford, Conn., in 1636, and married Elizabeth Watts in 1640. (He died March 18, 1685, at Middletown.) Robert Hubbard died at his residence in Long Hill Jan. 20, 1779, aged 66. His widow survived him many years, and died aged 92.

13*

Their children, born in Middletown, Long Hill, were:

Phebe, b. July, 1736, d. in infancy.

Elihu, b. Aug., 1737, d. 1770.

Abigail, b. Jan. 5, 1739, m. Dr. Smith.

Phebe 2d, b. Oct. 10, 1740, m. D. Wells.

Robert, b. March, 1742, d. in infancy.

Robert 2d, b. Sept., 1743, m. Lucy Hubbard (cousin).

Elijah, b. 1745, m. 1, H. Kent, 2, Abigail Dickinson.

Micah, b. 1747, d. in infancy.

Micah 2d, b. Sept. 8, 1748, m. Content Guernsey, of Durham.

Elizabeth, b. 1750, m. J. Morris.

Samuel, b. 1752.

MICAH HUBBARD.

Micah Hubbard, the sixth son of Robert Hubbard and Elisabeth Sill, was a great grandson of Elisabeth Hyde, of the third generation. He married Content Guernsey, of Durham, June 10, 1784. She was the eldest daughter of Lemuel Guernsey and Ruth Camp. He, Micah, settled at the old homestead of his father, Robert, in Long Hill. He died Dec. 1, 1731, aged 83 years. His widow survived him 17 years, and died at the advanced age of 92. Their children were Elihu, Ebenezer G., Ruth, Phebe, and Betsey. Phebe married Thomas Hubbard, of Utica, N. Y. They had several children: the rest died without issue. Micah Hubbard was a conscientious and upright man, and his views of religion were strictly Puritanical. He began the Christian Sabbath, or Lord's Day, at sunset Saturday night. At that time all labor ceased on his farm. A carpenter was making a hay cart for him, and he had almost got it done at sunset, Saturday— might have finished it before dark. He was ordered to stop work. The carpenter, whose name was Jacob, said he could finish the job and save coming Monday morning. Uncle Micah said: "Jacob, I am able to pay you for coming Monday morning, so put up your tools."

NOADIAH HUBBARD.

Noadiah Hubbard, the third son of Nathaniel Hubbard and Sarah Johnson (Nathaniel Hubbard, born Sept. 14, 1690, was son of Nathaniel the first, of Middletown, and Mary Earl, born Dec. 10, 1652,) who was the youngest son of George Hubbard, who was born in Wakefield, England, in 1594, and who came to Hartford in 1636, and in 1640 married Elisabeth Watts, daughter of Richard Watts. He first settled in Hartford. He left there in 1650, and came to Middletown, where he died March 18, 1865). Noadiah Hubbard settled at the old homestead. He married the widow of Levi Crowell, she having two children by her first husband—Levi and Eda.

Their children were:

Noadiah, who married a Ward and moved to

Steuben, N. Y., then called the "Black River Country."

Joel, —

Fairchild, —

Bela, —

Stephen, —

Samuel, who married a Crowell and lived on the homestead.

Phebe, —

JOHN HUBBARD.

John Hubbard, born in the year 1692, was an early settler in Long Hill. An old record in the Hubbard family makes him a descendant of George Hubbard, born in Yorkshire, England, in 1616, and fifth son of Nathaniel, born in 1652 (died 1738). John Hubbard, born 1692, was an early settler in Long Hill, yet we find no record of the exact time of his settlement. His house was probably built about the year 1733. There was no date in the old house, lately pulled down. The house stood at the foot of the hill on the old Durham road, a little south of the causeway. On the site of the old house a son of the late Jeremiah has erected an elegant residence (1872). There is an old Bible at the house with this inscription: "Stephen Hubbard, his Bible. Bought in New York by Elnathan Camp of Durham, for 22 shillings, their money, equal to 16 shillings and sixpence, lawful money, and one shilling lawful money for freight and commission, in all 1 £ 7s. 6d., lawful money, Dec., A. D. 1771."

The children of John Hubbard were Stephen, John, Jeremiah, Jabez, and two daughters, Mary and Elisabeth. Mary married Major Starr, and Elisabeth married and moved away.

JOHN CROWELL.

John Crowell the first was an early settler in Long Hill, Highlands. His house stood on the west side of the highway that divides the East and West School Districts. It stood nearly opposite the Elisha Fairchild house. This first Crowell house was built about the year 1738, and was taken down in 1838, and a new one built in its stead by a grandson, Comfort Crowell. John Crowell married a Bidwell, of Chatham. Little is known of the Crowells previous to their settlement in Middletown. They were of Dutch or German origin. The children of John the first were John the second, Daniel, Lewis, Abigail, and Mary. Lewis married a sister of Joel Fairchild. Abigail married Elisha Fairchild, who died of small-pox. The children of Abigail and Elisha Fairchild were Abigail, who married Abner Norton, of Durham; Olive, who married Daniel Southmayd, of Durham; Phebe, who married Thomas Burnham and moved to Hartland; and Elisha, who married Lucretia Tryon, of South Farms.

DANIEL CROWELL.

Daniel Crowell remained on the old place. He married Sarah Hubbard, born in Long Hill, Jan.

16, 1751. She was the oldest daughter of Nehemiah Hubbard and Sarah Sill, and granddaughter of Joseph Sill and Phebe Lord, of Lyme, Conn. Their children were:

Daniel 2d, b. April 4, 1772, moved to Hartford, Conn., 1797, d. July 17, 1867, something over 95 years old. His first wife was Sarah A. Olcott, who died January 8, 1812. His second wife was Lucy T. Dwight. She was born Aug. 29, 1794; died Oct. 25, 1875.

Matthew, d. in youth.

Seth, m. Sarah Birdsey.

David, m. Lucy Ward.

Comfort, m. P. M. Arnold.

Elisabeth (Betsey), m. S. Birdsey.

Sarah, m. E. Tryon.

All but Daniel, the oldest, lived and died in the town in which they were born. Comfort Crowell occupied the old homestead. He took down the old house in 1837, and built a new one on the site. He married P. M. Arnold about the time he built the new house. Their children were James and Ellen.

JOHN CROWELL 2D.

John Crowell, son of John the first, married in 17— Sarah Fairchild. His second wife was Widow Starr, and the third one Lucy Miller, widow of William Miller. He settled a quarter of a mile, or more, east of the stone school-house in the East District, Long Hill. His children were twelve in number:

Elijah, m. — Miller.   Huldah, m. S. Hubbard.
Samuel, m. S. Hall.   Ruth, m. — Pomeroy.
John, m. ——.   Hannah, m. — Hall.
Rhoda, m. — Brooks.   Mary.
Sarah, m. — Clark.   Lewis.
Mary, m. Jabez Barnes.

John Crowell, in his youth, was in the French war. He went to Canada, and was under Gen. Wolfe at the taking of Quebec; and when he was 90 years old " he could shoulder his gun and show how fields were won." In 1825 his son Elijah and his grandson Samuel put on an ox sled a little over four cords of walnut wood, and he, at the age of 90 years, drove the load into the city of Middletown. Matthew T. Russell bought the load of wood, which came to a little over $28.

SAMUEL CROWELL.

Samuel Crowell lived on the homestead of his father. He married Sarah Hall. Their children were all born at the homestead:

Levi, b. 1785, m. — Brooks.
Esther, b. 1787, m. — Brooks.
Samuel, b. 1789, m. Louisa Crowell.
Adah, b. 1792, m. Timothy Gilbert.
Hannah, b. 1795, unmarried.
Ruth, b. 1797, m. Daniel M. Crowell (cousin).
Sarah, b. 1801, m. W. Steuben.

John, died in childhood.

John 2d, died in his 21st year, unmarried.

Samuel Crowell left the old place in 1822, and moved to the "Hall house," wherein his wife was born. Elijah Crowell, his brother, came from Steuben, N. Y., or that vicinity, in 1822, and took up his abode on the old homestead. He took care of his aged father till his death. He built a house on the opposite side of the road, wherein he lived, and wherein he died in a good old age. His children were Sarah, Daniel, Louisa, and Heman. Heman died at the South.

SAUL CROWELL.

Saul Crowell, an early settler, lived in the Highlands of Long Hill, on the southernmost east and west road. Little is known of his family. He had a brother Edward. The house lot still holds his name, and some of his old apple trees are still standing. It is a lovely, sheltered spot in spring time, and the blue birds and the robins are early visitors to this calm, sunny place.

EDWARD CROWELL.

Edward Crowell, brother of Saul, or Solomon, lived near by on the same road. More is known of him. "He had been a soldier in his youth, and fought in famous battles." He was in the "French and Indian wars," and was at the storm-ing of Quebec under Gen. Wolfe. He was a man of great strength and power. He married twice. He had four children by his first wife—Joseph, Lucy, Fanny, and Mary. Joseph married and spent most of his days in Durham. Lucy married and lived in the city of Middletown till the latter part of her life, which she spent with her daughter at Haydenville, Mass. Mary married Camp Coe, of Middlefield, and died young. Fanny married a Leonard, and moved away. His children by his second wife were Jehiel, Edward, Adonijah, Henry, Clara, Rachel, Sarah, Chauncey. All married and scattered about. Once upon a time a couple of tramps came along through Long Hill, and left a young babe in the school-house, which stood a few rods north of the Nathaniel Hubbard house, on the old Durham road. Edward Crowell took the babe home and took care of it for some time. Subsequently John Crowell took the boy and brought him up. He proved a fine young man, and he married a daughter of the said Crowell. They moved into New York State, and raised a fine family of children.

JOHN CROWELL, Jr.

John Crowell, jr., married R. Starr. They had three children. He died at the old homestead of his father. He, the said John, was a blacksmith by trade, and had a shop at the place now called Zoar. It stood near the quarry. (This quarry was operated on by Erastus and Silas Brainerd about the year 1820. They did not make it a

14

profitable business. From here they went to the "Portland Quarries" and became wealthy.)

THE BARNES FAMILIES.

Little is known of the early history of those families that settled on the Barnes tract of land, on the west side of Long Hill. All but one family were descendants of Shamgar and Maybe Barnes. The writer knew some of these families, and gleaned some historic facts from Mary Barnes, in his boyhood days; and later from Dennis Lee, a grandchild of Amos Barnes, and from the widow of Captain Lathrop Lee, who was the daughter of Amos Barnes, and also from Jemima Barnes, the widow of Giles Barnes.

GILES BARNES

Settled upon the hill at the head of the Barnes tract on the west side of "Ezekiel's Brook" as it was then called, — now called "Laurel Brook," and on the road at the head of "Laurel Grove." He had a small farm and was a blacksmith, and got a good living. He was married and had several children by a first wife. The children married and moved into New York State. His second wife was Jemima Atkins, the third daughter of Thomas Atkins. Giles Barnes died of a tumor on the lower part of his face; his widow survived him several years, and died at the age of nearly ninety. The house is still standing, and is one of the oldest houses in the town. Just below was the house of

EZEKIEL BARNES.

He had a grist-mill near his house; this mill ceased grinding about the year 1804. This family had one son, whose name was Allen. He used to tell fortunes when a young man. The old people sold out what little they had, and moved with their son to New York State. Here Allen Barnes was converted and became a Methodist preacher. After this he was once on a visit to Middletown and preached one or two sermons in the old M. E. Church. Ezekiel had a small orchard on the side hill near his house. He had some early apples on a certain year and made a barrel of cider. Some boys knowing the fact— and boys at that time were as roguish as they are at the present day—went to the house, and found the cellar door open and could find nothing to draw the cider in. There was some stir overhead, and for fear the old man would get through the door, one of the boys held the door, while the other boys drew the cider in their *hats*, and when they had got away with the cider, the boy that held the door left and overtook them down in the "Laurel Grove," below where they drank the cider from their hats, with great satisfaction. This took place more than 100 years ago.

THOMAS BARNES.

Thomas Barnes lived farther south, on the North and South road. He had several children, boys and girls. He died in 1788. There now remains nothing to mark the place where the house stood save some oyster-shells, and some yellow lilies which have not been exterminated.

THOMAS BARNES, Jun.

Thomas Barnes, jun., and his sister Mary lived a little north of their father on the other side of road, in a house that was old and dilapidated, when the writer was a boy. Here Thomas raised a family of children: five sons and two daughters. The sons were:

Nathaniel,   Elijah,
Thomas,   Josiah.
Jonathan,

The daughters were, Sibil, and Mary. Sibil married a man by the name of Strong, and moved to the State of Ohio. Jonathan married a Geer of Staddle Hill; he lived and died in Middletown. Thomas died at the South. Nathaniel died in the city of Middletown; he was a cabinet-maker. Elijah died at Ashtabula, Ohio. Josiah, so far as the writer knows, may still be living in Ashtabula, Ohio. He was the youngest.

JOSEPH BARNES.

Joseph Barnes' house stood on the corner of the road leading to Middlefield center, on the south side of the road. Little is known of his family. He died in the Sugar House Prison, New York City. In the Revolution he was taken a prisoner at Fort Washington. He died from starvation and British inhumanity. (He was the comrade of Elisha Hubbard.) His house was left desolate 100 years ago.

AMOS BARNES.

Amos Barnes lived not far from the corner on the south side of the road leading into the south part of Middlefield. He was a quiet, unobtrusive man. One of his daughters married Calvin Hall, and one married Captain Lathrop Lee (they had eleven children). He died a little past middle age, and his widow lived to old age.

NEHEMIAH BARNES.

Nehemiah Barnes lived south, at the termination of the road near the swamp. He died a prisoner in the Revolutionary War. Perhaps in the British Prison Ship. The Barnes men were daring and good soldiers. They reckoned more upon getting a shot at a British Red-Coat than a hunter would at getting a shot at a flock of ducks or wild geese. A son of Nehemiah had his eyes accidentally shot out when young. He lived many years after this sad event.

JABEZ BARNES.

Jabez Barnes settled near the old school-house, West Long Hill. He was not a near relative of the other Barnes families. He married Martha, the second daughter of Thomas Atkins, in 1758. (She was a granddaughter of Benjamin ("Gov.")

14*

Miller, one of the first settlers of Middlefield, Conn. Jabez Barnes was a sailor, and died at sea, leaving a family of eight children. These children were:

Daniel, who married and moved to Steuben, N. Y.

Ithamar, who married and moved to Roxbury, Mass.

Jabez, who married a Crowell and moved to the "Black River Country."

Elizur, married a Bacon, and lived and died in Middletown, Conn.

Levi, who married and moved to the "Black River Country."

Elisha, married a Plum and lived and died in Middletown.

Abiah, married Moses Lucas, moved to Phelpstown in old age.

Martha, who married a Lee. She died young, leaving three children: Daniel, Eliza, and Mary.

Martha Barnes, the wife of Jabez Barnes, and the mother of these eight children, was a wonderful woman of the age in which she lived. Left with this family of children, a one-story house, a small barn, and eight or ten acres of land, she managed to take care of her children until they became old enough to take care of themselves. She took in weaving and worked early and late, and yet she found time to go to church, and used to walk to meeting two miles and a half, on

Sabbath days when she was past middle age. She was an eminently religious woman, of great courage, and of strong common sense. A pencil sketch of her was made by some young relative, as she sat reading the Bible at the advanced age of 96. (This sketch has been reproduced with pen and ink until it is found in many families connected with her in Middletown, Conn.)

The following anecdote will illustrate her true, go-ahead character. She wanted to purchase some necessary articles for her family. She rode on horseback into the city of Middletown, and among other things she bought a "sheep's head and pluck." She put the meat into a bag and laid it over the fence in the yard of Timothy Southmayd, a little south of the "Savings Bank" of Middletown. A man seeing her drop the bag over the fence, went and took it up, and marched off with it in the absence of the owner. When Mrs. Barnes came back for her bag she found that it was gone. She made inquiry and learned that a man was seen going toward the "Farms" with a bag on his back. She put the whip to the horse and started on a jump after the man. She met "Captain Clay" as she turned the "Clay Corner," and asked him if a man had passed that way with a bag on his back. "Yes," said he, "and he is now just over the Causeway Bridge." She replied "he has stolen my bag and I mean to rawhide him." She started on his track over the bridge, and came up with him about half-way up the hill. Seeing the mark on the bag, and knowing it was hers, she saluted him, "You dog, you have stole my pluck!" at the same time she drew the whip over his head and shoulders. He dropped the bag and ran for the fence, but not before he had received a pretty good castigation from her muckle hand. Captain Clay followed on as fast as he could, to be ready, if there was any resistance, to help the woman. A short sketch of the life of Martha Barnes was written and published in 1834 by Rev. J. Cookson of the Baptist Church. She died in 1834, aged ninety-six years.

THE CORNWELL FAMILIES.

CAPTAIN WAIT CORNWELL'S

House stood some way up from the road that divided the Barnes and Cornwell tracts of land. It faced the West. The road was much traveled by the early settlers of Durham and Middlefield, and this is shown by the deep ruts cut in the rocks where the wheels passed over. Time changed the tide of travel, and the old Durham road east of this section became the main traveled road from Hartford and Middletown, through Durham to New Haven. Long after the Cornwell house was built was the road cut through the land east, to unite with the Durham road. The Cornwell house is the oldest in Long Hill, and is now in good condition. It was built by Captain Wait Cornwell about the year 1723.

He was the seventh child of Jacob Cornwell, and Mary White of the First Society, Middletown. The house, as originally built, was forty feet long and twenty wide, two stories high, with a lintel or "lean to" roof some twelve or fifteen feet wide, and of the same length as the main building, and one story high. The posts and timber in the house are all of oak, and of great size and strength. The corner posts of the second story are eighteen inches square, and the beams proportionately large. The cellar was under only a part of the house. This was the style of building at that time, and still later, among the early settlers. Little is known about the children of Wait Cornwell the first. There were sons and daughters. His son Timothy inherited the homestead, and most of the farm. He was an old man, when well remembered by the writer of this history. His wife was a cripple in the latter part of her life, and used to roll around the room in a chair to do her work. They both died within a few years of each other, and were buried in the "Farm Hill" burying ground. Their children were, from the best accounts : Timothy, Wait, and a daughter. It is supposed that the daughter married a man by the name of Lee. Timothy died young. Wait Cornwell was sent to Yale College, where he graduated in 1795 or thereabout. He was an ordained Presbyterian preacher, and had a charge on Long Island for a time. He came home and attended Baptist meetings at Mr. Doolittle's at Staddle Hill, and became a warm Calvinistic Baptist and was immersed in the river, the north side of the bridge, a little east of the grist-mill.

FRANCIS CORNWELL.

Francis Cornwell, "an old man-of-wars-man," settled early on the Cornwell tract of land, about one-third of a mile south of Captain Wait Cornwell's. He built a one-story house. Here he lived rather poor and discontented to old age—he died in 1806, or near that time. His wife survived him some years, and died in 1816 or 1817. Their children were: Nathaniel, Louis, ——, and Betty. Francis Cornwell went to sea in a merchant vessel, and was pressed on board a British man-of-war, and was detained six years in the prime of life. One cold winter's night the old man went across the swamp east of his house, the ground being frozen hard, and took from his neighbor's fence a long pole. The owner, Jabez Hubbard, was just returning home from chopping wood, and seeing the pole move off the fence, hastened along and took hold of the other end of the pole before the old man had got out of the bushes. He gave a surge, thinking the pole was entangled in the bushes, the owner let go, and after a few steps took hold of the end of the pole again with the same result. The third time the old man looked around, and seeing the owner at the end of the pole, threw it off from his shoulder to the ground. They parted, each to his own house, without exchanging a word. The pole lay there till spring, when it was put back on the fence.

ATKINS.

The name in New England first appears as copied from an old record :

    " Joseph Atkins of Roxbury (Mass.), married
        a Dudley in the year 1630.

    " Abraham Atkins, Boston, 1642.

    " Matthew Atkins, Boston (Freeman), 1673.

    " Thomas Atkins (brother of Josiah), Hart-
        ford, East River, married 1688.

    " Thomas Atkins, Boston (Freeman), 1690."

JOSIAH ATKINS.

Josiah Atkins (brother of Thos.), married Elizabeth, daughter of Thos. Wetmore, Sen., of Middletown, Oct. 8, 1673. Children :

1. Sarah Atkins, born July 16, 1674.
2. Abigail (married Robert Hubbard), born Sept. 11, 1676.
3. Solomon, born July 25, 1678.
4. Josiah, born March 9, 1680.
5. Benjamin, born Nov. 19, 1682.
6. Ephraim, born March 9, 1685.
7. Elizabeth (married Ward, Haddam), born Aug. 11, 1687.

"The town gave him four acres of meadow land near Robert Johnson's farm, next to John

Stow, Sen's., land. Josiah Atkins died Sept. 12, 1690. Will, March 1, 1690, inventory made Jan. 1, 1691. Estate, £67 10s."

EPHRAIM ATKINS.

" Ephraim Atkins (son of Josiah Atkins), married Elizabeth Wetmore, daughter of Thomas Wetmore, Jun., June 16, 1709." Children :

1. Thomas, born Apr. 5, 1710.
2. Ephraim (died young), July 18, 1712.
3. Elizabeth (died May 30, 1750), born Dec. 6, 1714.
4. Ephraim, born March 22, 1717.
5. Naomi, born June 6, 1719.
6. Eleazer, born Oct. 1, 1721.
7. James, born Apr. 9, 1724.
8. George, born Dec. 26, 1726.

Ephraim Atkins, Sen., died Dec. 26, 1760. Elizabeth, his wife died May 20, 1752. Ephraim bought his land in N. Long Hill of John Brown (near College, Wesleyan), in 1708.

(The Atkins family came from England.)

THOMAS ATKINS.

Thomas, the oldest son of Ephraim Atkins, was born Apr. 5, 1710. He was an early settler in Long Hill. He married Martha Miller, daughter of Benjamin Miller (called " Gov. Miller "), who lived at Cauginchaug, now Middlefield, Ct. His marriage took place in June, 1735. He built a house on the old Durham road in 1734, his land adjoining Nathaniel Hubbard's on the north. The house stood a few rods northwest of the brick house built by Ithamar Atkins in 1807, afterward owned and occupied by his son Albert Atkins (and at present by his grandson, Thomas J. Atkins). The children of Thomas and Martha Miller Atkins were:

Mary, b. Dec. 20, 1736, m. Joshua Miller.

Martha, b. July 17, 1739, m. Jabez Barnes.

Jemima, b. Oct. 13, 1741, m. Giles Barnes.

Sarah, b. Oct. 27, 1745, m. Phineas Bacon.

Lydia, b. Nov. 23, 1747, m. Edward Ward.

Rhoda, born Jan. 15, 1749, married J. Ward.

Lucy, b. Apr. 28, 1752, m, 1. — Johnson; 2. — Coe.

Ithamar, the eighth child, b. Nov. 16, 1757, m. Anna Hubbard (she was the twelfth child of Nehemiah Hubbard, and granddaughter of Nathaniel Hubbard, and was born Oct. 18, 1762).

Thomas Atkins was a quiet, good-natured man, honest in his dealings. His wife was a stout, courageous woman, a good representative of her father (Benjamin Miller). They lived "in days that tried men's souls." She could not bear the name of "tory." When she was in her ninety-third year, a gentleman called at her house, and to see if she retained, at this advanced age, the same hatred to tories that she did during the war of the Revolution, it was proposed that the man should assume to be a

15

tory, and this should be made known to the old
lady. No sooner was she informed that the man
in the other room was suspected of being a tory,
than she armed herself with a broomstick, entered
the room and ordered the man out of the house.
Not obeying the demand directly, she attempted
to strike him over the head, repeating, "I will
not have a tory in my house," he defending himself, and retreating towards the door before this
formidable weapon.

'Twas good to learn of her what freedom cost,
  What trials all passed through, what bitter tears were shed
For those who fought at Lexington, and those who lost
  Their lives on Bunker Hill, where youthful Warren bled.
When more than ninety years had thinned her snowy hair,
  And time had deeply worn its furrows on her brow,
She could not then, the sight or name of " tory," bear,
  For "liberty or death " was still her solemn vow.

ITHAMAR ATKINS.

Ithamar Atkins, the eighth child of Thomas
Atkins, settled on the old homestead. He
married Anna Hubbard, Nov. 27, 1783. She
was the twelfth child of Nehemiah Hubbard
and Sarah Sill, and granddaughter of Nathaniel
Hubbard and Sarah Johnson. The children of
Ithamar and Anna were :

Jacob, b. Dec. 26, 1786, m. Mary Miller
  (daughter of Jacob Miller, Middlefield).
Rhoda, b. June 11, 1790, died unmarried.
Richard, b. Aug. 29, 1792, m. Malinda
  Edwards.
Maria, b. March 23, 1795, m. Augustus
  Philips and moved to Ithaca, New York.

Thomas, b. March 4, 1797, m. Lucy Miller.

Sarah, b. Apr. 19, 1799, died unmarried.

Henry, m. Sarah B. Crowell, } twins, b. Jan.
William H., m. Eliza Powers, } 11, 1801.

Albert, born Sept. 14, 1804, m Susan E. Hale.

Ithamar Atkins was a man of sound judgment and strong reasoning powers. He used to have many conflicts with his neighbor, Priest Wait Cornwell. Cornwell was a rigid Calvinistic Baptist, and once in the recollection of the author of this history, the two were hotly engaged in discussing the doctrine of election and reprobation. Atkins asked him what he thought would be the fate of children dying in infancy. He replied, there might be a certain portion of them damned and sent to hell. "Well," says Atkins, "that is damnable doctrine." Cornwall says, "I won't hear you talk." "I tell you to hear me," was the reply. "I *won't* hear you," said he, "it is false what you say, and it is false *what you are going to say*"!

JESSE ATKINS.

Jesse Atkins settled on the south part of Long Hill on the old Durham road. Little is known of him in his early days. It is probable that he was a descendant of Dea. Solomon Atkins. Some of his children were known to the writer. Jesse, Samuel, and William,—there may have been more. Jesse lived on the homestead. Samuel lived on the cross-road a little east of the Durham road, and William still farther east on the road. Jesse sold out to Daniel or Seth Crowell, and moved down on the cross-road near the "Field Brook" (a branch of the Pameachy), where he died about the year 1808. His children were, Elisha and Olive.

WILLIAM ATKINS.

William Atkins, son of Jesse, married Mitty Clover. Their children were : William, Stephen, Luman, and two or three daughters. His wife died and he married again, and had one son by the second marriage. He sold his place, and moved into New York State about 1824. Samuel Atkins second, a son of Samuel the first, lived on the homestead. He sold out to —— Hubbard and moved to Harwinton, Conn. Seth settled north of the homestead a short distance. He sold out and moved to the town of Lee, Mass.

WARDS.

The Wards were early settlers in Long Hill, East District. They settled not far from the old stone school-house. One a little east down the hill ; the other on the road south, near the termination of the "Wall Rocks." They were descendants of John Ward and William Ward. John and William were landholders in Middletown in 1670. The Wards came from Rowley, Mass., to Middletown. The children of John Ward second, were : John, third, who married a

Newton of Durham; George, who married a Smith, and built a house north of the old homestead, on the corner lot; Sarah, who married D. Crowell, and died in middle life of cancer. George sold his place and moved into New York State. John sold his farm in 1831, and moved into N. Y., but came back and bought the Brooks place on Farm Hill, where he died in old age.

JOHN WARD.

John Ward the first was a large landholder. He owned a section of land forty rods wide, extending to the Durham line. His house stood on the north part of this section. He had another section farther East. The "Fenno Roberts" house stood on the north part of this section. It is understood that Josiah Ward, who lived at the "Sand Hill," was not a near connection of John Ward's family. The "Sand Hill" family of Ward sold out and moved to the "Black River Country" about the year 1813. Some of the family had gone before.

JONATHAN GILBERT.

Jonathan Gilbert settled early in Long Hill. His house was built about the year 1738. He died in 1805, aged 97 years. His house stood between the house of Nehemiah Hubbard, and the Laurel Grove, on a knoll on the west side of the road. It was pulled down in 1825 or thereabout. His children were: Jonathan, 2d, Ezekiel,

15*

Martha, who married —— Cornwell. One daughter married —— Powers, and one married a Nancar. Jonathan settled on the homestead. He married a daughter of Daniel Wetmore. His children were: Daniel, Horace, Collins, Sarah, Prudence, Hannah, Maria, Lucy, and Julia. Jonathan sold out his farm, etc., and in 1816 or '17, moved west to the State of Ohio, that part called "New Connecticut." The Gilbert family were naturally courteous and polite, and fond of company. The old man was a witty and shrewd man. He was rigidly Puritanical. One of his daughters married a Powers. They were among the first Methodists in the city of Middletown. The old gentleman asked his son-in-law how he could afford to entertain so many Methodist preachers. His son replied that they did not eat or drink much. "Then," said the old man, "they have got to the right place."

MOSES LUCAS.

Moses Lucas was an early settler in Long Hill. His house was a one-story dwelling, and stood on the east side of the road that divided the Clark tract of land from the Wards and Hubbards, about one-third of a mile south, from the road running east and west by the stone school-houses. The house stood not far from the brook. (This road divides the two school districts. Those persons living on the west side of the road, belong to the West District, those living on the

east side belong to the East District.) Moses
Lucas the first, came from the First Society.
Little is known of his early history, only that
several Lucas families were among the early
settlers of Middletown, Ct. Moses Lucas erected
his house, which was one-story high, about the
year 1735. We know not whom he married for
his first wife. In our remembrance he had a
second wife. His children were: Moses 2d,
Thomas, Elnathan, Noah (who was lost at sea),
Asenath, and Abigail. Moses 2d, married Abiah
Barnes (granddaughter of Thos. Atkins), and
settled on the homestead. His children were:
Eber, Ruth, Jabez, Abiah, and Horace. He sold
out to Elisha Barnes in 1818, and moved with
his family to Phelpstown, N. Y.

Moses Lucas the first, displayed great ingenuity
in telling unique and curious stories. (Perhaps
this historian will be pardoned for relating some
of them.) Some one once made the remark in
his hearing, that he never knew so sudden a
change in the weather from heat to cold. He
replied that he once knew a change in the
weather so sudden that the frogs in a pond near
his house had not time to draw down their
heads, they were all sticking up above the ice,
and he went along shortly after on the pond and
kicked off half a bushel of frogs' heads. (?)
Speaking of quick cattle, he said he once had a
pair of oxen so quick and powerful, that they
drew a load of hay from the "Boggy Meadows"

ahead of a thunder shower, and it rained so hard that his dog swam all the way home behind his cart, his hay not getting wet at all. (?)   Wild pigeons were quite thick in his day, and he used to tell the story of a shot he once made at a large flock of pigeons, which started up from a field of buckwheat stubble.   He said he fired at this immense flock without killing one pigeon, but on examining the ground, he found that he had shot just under them and had cut off more than a bushel basket full of legs. (?)   He said he once had a field of rye, so stout and thick, that a black snake ran across the whole field on top of the heads. (?)

THOMAS LUCAS.

Thomas Lucas married a Gillum of Durham, and after his marriage, for many years, he lived on the Elijah Hubbard farm on the old Durham road, a mile or two south of the city of Middletown.   Here he raised a large family.   His children were: Noah, Elijah, Amos, Thomas, George and Julia (twins), and Levi.   He had a fit of sickness which left him in a deranged state of mind.   He drew a pension in the latter part of his life, for services in the Revolution.   He died of small-pox in 18—.

JOHN BLAKE.

John Blake was an early settler in Long Hill. His house was located on high and broken land in the East School District, south of the Ward place. Little is known of his family except that he had a daughter by the name of Nabby, and she married a man by the name of Tryon. Nabby Blake had a spring of water not far from her house, wherein she used to put her cream to cool it, previous to churning. Some roguish boys came that way, and seeing the pail of cream in the spring, took off the cover and put in the pail a large frog. It was said that the frog in jumping around to get out of his creamy prison, actually churned the butter, and that Aunt Nabby, when she came for her pail of cream, found the frog sitting on the cake of butter and looking as demure as a country justice. John Blake, the father of Nabby, was once tied up to an apple-tree and whipped by some of his neighbors, because he voted in opposition to their wishes at a "Freeman's meeting." He made complaint to Dr. Dickinson, who was then a "justice of the peace." The judge took no notice of it, farther than to say that they served him right. Mr. Blake thought it uncommon hard to be tied to his own apple-tree and whipped for voting as he thought best, and no redress to be obtained.

FREELOVE BLAKE.

Freelove Blake was an old settler in the highlands of Long Hill. We have no data of the exact time of his settlement. It was not far from 1760. He built a small one-story house in a wild place on the east side of the north and south road. The "Wall Rocks" was the eastern boundary of his home-lot, where was the famous "snake hole." Here he lived to old age, and seemed to enjoy life. He had quite a family of children; one is living at this time (1878), and is upwards of 90 years old. Contentment makes a home pleasant anywhere, and this man seemed content in this lonely place of abode. High rocks and woody hills environed his humble dwelling, and it is presumed that he never saw the morning sun till it was an hour or two high, or the gold and crimson sunset, unless he was away from home. His children were: Reuben, George, Richard, Nancy, and Betsey. Some might have died in infancy or childhood. He believed that black snakes were gifted with the power of charming birds. The writer heard him tell the following story, more than seventy years ago. He said that he was out in the lot, not far from his house, when he saw a bird flying round and round in great distress. To use his own words—"I sought the cause, and found that a large black snake had complete control of the bird. I stepped back and procured a pole and marched up to a proper distance from the snake, as I thought, when I struck a most *pernicious* blow, but it fell short of the snake. The next time I measured my steps, killed the snake at the second blow, and released the bird."

DWELLING-HOUSES.

The number of houses in the East district has not varied much for more than a half century, only near the city line, and around the factories. There are now (1878) in East Long Hill, thirty-seven dwelling-houses.

WEST LONG HILL.

The number of houses in the West district (1878) is forty-six, exclusive of the "Industrial School Buildings." Not much increase in the houses in the district for a long time, unless it be near the city limit or near the factories. Some Irish houses have sprung up in the highlands of Long Hill, while others of the old settlers have long since disappeared.

INDEX.

16